THE SECRET ORPHAN SISTERS

Rivka Kan-Tor (Hershkowitz)

Production by eBookPro Publishing
www.ebook-pro.com

THE SECRET ORPHAN SISTERS
Rivka Kan-Tor (Hershkowitz)

Translation from Hebrew: Seree Zohar
Editing: Nancy Alroy

Contact: tsvi@ktalegal.com

ISBN 9798345722923

The Secret Orphan Sisters

*A WWII historical fiction novel
based on a true story*

RIVKA KAN-TOR (HERSHKOWITZ)

*This book is dedicated to the
memories of my dear parents and family,
murdered in the Holocaust.*

Contents

INTRODUCTION

There is no end to these memories, nor any way to erase them.

They may be shunted aside due to life's demands, but they resurface in various circumstances: for example, the evening of my marriage.

What tremendous joy! But I can't help looking for my parents among the attendees. Where's my mother to lead me to the marriage canopy? Tears pour from my eyes. Everyone thinks I'm crying for joy, as most brides do at their wedding. But I'm not crying: I'm crying out. My heart is screaming for my parents, and they do not hear, they do not see. I'm about to be married! Where are you?

They resurface in my dreams. Forty-five years have passed since the war but I still have those dreams. They may appear once a month, once in two to three months, but the dream is always clear and in sharp focus, as though the events occurred yesterday.

On one occasion I see my mother's eyes gazing at me for the last time, just before the Germans forcibly separated us. In another dream I'm still in the concentration camp, dogs chasing me. I hear them barking, and I'm afraid. And within the dream itself, I ask myself: am I dreaming or is this real? Then I scream for help. Sometimes I see myself escaping, but I never manage to get to a safe place. I run and run until I've run out of strength. Then I scream or call out, but my voice can't make a sound. I choke.

Nightmares like these have continued for a great many years. I'd wake from them covered in sweat. My dear husband, Moshe, would hug me close, trying to calm me until, eventually, I'd relax and fall back to sleep.

Over time, the frequency of dreams became sporadic but it seems they'll never disappear altogether. For years I didn't speak of the Holocaust; the subject wasn't open for discussion and I didn't want to touch upon it. Suddenly one day, everything erupted like a storm and memories flooded me, stunning me with their force. Reliving them, it's hard to imagine how they'd been preserved in my mind.

Once again I see the wide-open staring eyes begging for help. I hear the cries at night and catch the stench of burning bodies. I see the red smoke flaring up from chimneys of the Auschwitz-Birkenau crematoria.

Sometimes I can't help wondering: was that really me? Or perhaps my doppelganger who experienced the horrors?

Forty-five years: that's how long I've waited to write this book.

I had no idea how to start, or when it would end.

I just knew that, from the moment I began, the book wrote itself: the memories burst forth and flowed.

Write! a powerful voice within me demanded.

Write and tell it all!

Write about the Holocaust that our people experienced.

Write about the six million, tortured, killed, burned alive, all innocent.

I have come to feel it my duty to document the events I underwent, the horrors I saw in the Holocaust, the fears, the sights and voices which never leave me. Nightmares, fears, and the raucous sound of barking dogs still accompany me. There can never be forgiveness or reconciliation over the genocide of my people.

And so I must write:

For the sake of my family, murdered in Auschwitz.

For the sake of my friends, assisting each other through our harshest hours, many of whom never survived.

For the sake of my children, grandchildren, and the generations to follow, with the caveat that, even though time continues to pass since the days of concentration camps, the past should never be forgotten.

I've never written a book before but I knew deep in my heart that, even if the pages I write yellow over time in a cupboard, I still need to tell these stories that have become an integral part of who I am and have accompanied me throughout my life.

I've done my best to maintain a normal family life, but it's futile to rid my mind of the memories, expel from the sights of the past from my eyes, or my heart to overcome the loss of my family.

It was a kind of madness that demands to be recorded.

Detail after detail surfaces; one event after another.

How often have I've asked myself whether the events that took place in the camps really happened to me, or perhaps they are from some previous incarnation, and I revisited them as a resurrected being?

THE HOUSE IN VELKA SEVLUŠ

I was born in Sevluš, known in Yiddish as 'Selish,' a city at the foothills of the Carpathian mountains in Czechoslovakia. Sevluš was a quiet, pretty city, the capital of the district known for its grapes and strawberries that were distributed to all the larger cities. The city is now called Vynohradiv and is situated in western Ukraine.

Every Thursday the large market had the very best on offer: villagers brought fruit and vegetables, chickens, ducks and geese, and so much more.

The city's large hospital served the population of Sevluš and its surrounds. There was also a vocational school and a municipal high school where gentiles and Jews studied together.

At home we kept the Jewish traditions, strictly observing Shabbat and festivals in accordance with Jewish law. The synagogue provided assistance to the needy, visits to the ill, distribution of matzah for Passover to those who had financial hardship, donations to assist newlyweds, and so on. Sevluš Jews attended synagogue as a matter of course.

The city's Jewish population was comprised of merchants, craftsmen, flour millers, clerks, lumber traders, and landowners, all facing the daily struggle of providing for their families and trying to live peaceably with our non-Jewish neighbors.

As children, we spoke four or five languages: Yiddish with our parents, calling them Tateh and Mameh rather than Papa and Mama; Hungarian with our childhood friends and other children we played with in the street; and at school we studied Russian, Czechoslovak, and Ukrainian. Interestingly, we never thought twice about switching from one language to another.

Ours was a family of seven children: six girls and one boy. I was the sixth girl and, to my sorrow, don't remember my older sisters very well, nor my only brother. There was a large age gap between us, and my memories are mostly from photos and their brief visits home during vacations or for the Jewish holidays.

My sister Rozie married when she was 19, leaving the house to join her husband Zoli Adler in Bratislava, Slovakia, where their son Moshe, nicknamed Miki, was born. My brother Zeril-Hersh left home at the age of 15 to study at the Komárno Yeshiva in Slovakia. At 18 he also traveled to Bratislava, where he worked during the day and completed his high school studies in the evenings. My sister Feigie studied sewing in Sevluš and at 19 joined Rozie, working in Bratislava as a fashion salon seamstress. She loved sports and excelled in skiing and ice skating. My sister Goldie wanted to study business and economics but, by then, Jews were no longer allowed to attend institutes of higher learning. Instead, she decided to move to Budapest. Hannah, another sister, found herself facing the same problem and, at 18, joined Goldie in Budapest.

This reminds me of a story often told at home, perhaps in jest, perhaps half seriously. When the oldest, Rozie Rachel, was born, someone immediately came to my father's shop to give him the wonderful news. In those days it was customary for midwives to assist in delivery at home. Tateh was very pleased, shut the shop, and quickly made his way home. The next child was a boy, Zeril-Hersch. Once again someone went to the shop to inform him, he shut the store and ran home. A son, after all!

The third was a girl, Feigie-Tzipporah, the fourth a girl, Goldie-Zahava. When someone came to inform my father of his daughter's birth, this was said to be his reaction: "Fine, fine. Mazel tov. What's all the fuss over? I'll be home soon." When the fifth was born, a girl named Hannah, he reacted in the same way. When another daughter, Hilda-Rivka, the sixth, was born, the same reaction. But when little Sheindy-Yaffa was born, Tateh apparently said: "Enough! Six girls! No more attempts for another son!"

We lived in a private home with a yard and plot of land. Beyond the yard was a garden planted with fruit trees. They were Tateh's pride and joy. On the plot we grew row upon row of bright red, fragrant and plump strawberries. Roses in all kinds of colors also grew there, some climbing over the fence separating the yard from the garden. Grape vines flourished in the yard, loaded with heavy clusters of white, black and red grapes, delectable to eye and palate.

Our home was always open to friends and neighbors. Aunts, uncles and cousins would come to visit on Shabbat afternoons and we'd spend many pleasant hours together.

Although there was a Beit Yakov Hebrew School in the city, many of the Jewish children attended the municipal school together with the non-Jewish children. I remember excursions we made on foot with the class: to Teplice, with its healing baths and fountains; to the Tisza River, which wasn't far from our home; and to Kankó and the Kankó-vár castle on the mountaintop. I also remember getting together with my girlfriends and going to the cinema to see the films starring little Shirley Temple as well as Johnny Weismuller's Tarzan.

On summer vacations, Mameh, Sheindy and I would visit the village of Kaposvár where my father was born and where his sister, my aunt, ran a guest house. People would come from near and far because of the healing springs. Boiling mineral water and springs would erupt from the earth, curing all kind of illnesses and conditions. Others simply enjoyed the spa experience.

Visiting Kaposvár was always fun; we loved being there. We made many friends with children from the village's and would go with them for walks through the fields, picking red currants from the bushes scattered everywhere and arranging plays to the delight of the adults.

We were happy in the village. We made plans, dreamed, and the world looked rosy. Two weeks of vacation would pass faster than the blink of an eye. When we left, it was always with the hope that we'd be back the next year, but 1943 was the last of those vacations.

One day a rumor spread that trains were passing through our city, their carriages crammed with Jews heading to Poland and, from there, to an unknown destination. Sevluš' Jews organized to bring food to our fellow Jews trapped in trains that had stopped at the station but weren't letting anyone off.

Back home, life continued as normal, but signs of the oncoming Holocaust were starting to show. Jews were dismissed from their places of employment, licenses to owners of businesses were revoked, and orders were given not to trade with Jews. Universities were closed to Jewish students. Basically all rights were cancelled vis-à-vis Jews but, because these decrees were implemented in stages, the Jewish residents continued to hope that things would take a turn for the better. They clung to the illusion that these signs were no more than black clouds which would soon disperse; no one could imagine the catastrophe that was taking great strides to reach us.

Back then it was common for the 'municipal drummer' to convey information. A policeman would begin drumming, and residents young and old, Jewish and gentile, would gather around to hear what he had to say. The town crier would appear ringing his bell two or three times a day, and every announcement brought with it more restrictions on the Jewish community, to the joy of the gentiles.

Our street held a mix of Jewish and non-Jewish residents. To all appearances, neighborly relations pervaded but, beneath the surface, hatred bubbled; and when these decrees hit us, our non-Jewish neighbors and friends suddenly disappeared from view. Overnight they broke their connections with us, waiting for the moment when they could take our homes and freely loot our possessions. At that time in 1942, young Jewish men were recruited for forced labor, mostly digging ditches and building barricades. They were away from their homes for long months, some never returning. Most of those who remained at home were women, elderly men, children and the ill. Jews were still able to walk through streets freely, but the atmosphere was tense.

A decree was published in April 1944 ordering all Jews to wear the yellow patch on their clothes. Wherever we went, non-Jews pointed at us: "Here, look, the Jews." Every day brought new announcements, troubles and restrictions. The Germans exercised tight control and the gendarmes, our police, carried out their orders. They would catch Jews in the street and cut off the elderly Orthodox men's *peyot*, the long side-curls they grew in keeping with the biblical commandment. They forced these older men to dig pits and sweep streets and mocked them in every way possible. Beatings were abundant.

The next stage saw the complete separation of Jews from everyone else. The Germans closed off a section of the city facing the Great Synagogue, and concentrated the city's Jews there. The process of ghettoization began on the first day of the Jewish festival of Pessach (Passover), which fell on Friday, April 7, 1944. Our family packed a bit of food and some clothing. Several families were forced to cram into one apartment.

The Law of Expulsion applied to all Jews other than a number of families whose men had fought in the Austro-Hungarian army in WWI, had been injured, and were considered disabled veterans. Because my father had been wounded and had additionally received a military award acknowledging his excellence in active combat, our family was not deported and we were not required to wear the yellow chest patch. In retrospect, we were free, a lone family among a street full of non-Jews. The authorities issued us special documents allowing us to move freely around the city.

But the gentiles in our neighborhood did not understand why we enjoyed preferential treatment, and would harass us with various and odd questions. We would leave the house only for the purpose of buying groceries, limiting ourselves as much as possible to avoid garnering attention. One day the gendarmes showed up, informing us that the laws had been changed and, according to the newest edict, only Tateh was protected by the authorities. This meant that he was entitled to stay at home but we, his family, would have to move to the ghetto immediately.

What terrible news. Tateh was out at the time. Mameh offered the gendarmes alcoholic drinks as a way to buy time. They drank their first cup, drank a second, downed a third, and still Tateh hadn't returned. The gendarmes were not willing to wait any longer. Having no other choice, we packed several items and, with heavy hearts, went to the ghetto without even saying goodbye to him.

Once Tateh found out from the neighbors what had happened, he immediately traveled to Budapest to ascertain his rights with the authorities. The journey itself was extremely risky, but he was desperate enough to try anything. Eventually he returned with an order to release us from the ghetto unconditionally. That lit a spark of hope among the Jews in the ghetto: maybe, just maybe, they thought, the law will be changed and all of us will be released to our homes? Was this a sign of a better future on the horizon?

THE SAFE

In our home there were two closets, each slightly different from the other. Entering the house following our release from the ghetto, Tateh decided to prepare a hiding place, a kind of safe to store money and valuables. He pulled the shoes drawer out from one of the closets, shortened it by ten centimeters, and placed cash, deeds, share certificates and jewelry into the nook. Then he closed the space with a strip of wood and put the drawer back and the closet looked as it always had. I stood next to him while he worked. He explained that he hid the valuables there for emergencies.

"The day will come when we'll need it," he said. He wanted us all to know where the hiding place was. Then we went out to the garden, where Tateh dug a hole at a distance of two paces from the gate at the garden's furthest end, and pulled a wad of cash from his pocket. He placed them in a tin box and buried the tin for safekeeping.

After the war I told my sister Hannah the whole story. While we were in Budapest she decided to visit our parents' home and search for the treasure. It turned out that after we left the house for the second time and were made to reenter the ghetto, neighbors broke in and took the closet, never knowing what secret treasures were hidden behind the shoes drawer.

And what of the treasure in the tin box buried in the garden? Hannah walked around the trees, looking for where to dig in the garden and retrieve our box. But the people living in the house at the time, our former friends and neighbors, feared that my sister had returned to claim her property and were downright hostile towards her, hovering about and waiting for her to leave. Hannah decided not to reveal anything to them.

The family kept this secret. Who knows if the box isn't still hidden in the garden?

***

Our happiness at being back home didn't last long. Some days later the gendarmes were back, bearing an order that voided Tateh's preferential rights in entirety. Once again we were banished to the ghetto. When the Germans forced us to leave our home in Sevluš, our family was just two parents and two sisters: Sheindy, my younger sister, aged thirteen, and me, older by two years.

We took some clothing and left the house as it was, its contents intact. I left my memories there, my joyful years, my childhood. Would I ever live in the house again? Would I play in the yard I loved so much? Would I see our beautiful garden once more?

I gazed repeatedly at the items in my room, as though wanting to seal their images in my soul. I choked back tears until I couldn't. Out in the yard, my heart bid farewell to the trees, flowers and strawberries. There was no time for more than that. The gendarmes were pressuring us: you need to go, you need to hurry. It was as though I was rooted to the spot. Tateh, sensing my distress, came over, placed his hand on my shoulder, and led me silently around to the front yard. Looking up at him, I saw a tear rolling down his cheek.

Neighbors, our 'good friends,' coveting our home for a long time now, lurked outside as though waiting for prey, ready to invade and settle themselves inside. True, they promised to look after the home until we returned, but who at the time had any idea where we were going, and when we'd be back? We walked out of our home leaving everything as it was: breakfast on the table, pots on the stove, and organized our departure. Tateh said we had come to an end, that we wouldn't be back. He gave my sister and me some money, just in case, and we sewed it into our coats' shoulder pads. That's because Tateh said that if our clothes get taken from us, too, we won't be needing the money. He had no idea how right he would be. One of the gendarmes asked Mameh for the keys to lock the house. Mameh refused him, and locked the door herself, handing the keys to him afterwards.

We stepped out into the street. Mameh and Tateh held hands, gazing back through tearful eyes at the house where they'd raised seven children, the house which now seemed abandoned, silent. It broke their hearts to see their life's work taken from them. We set off, a strange procession of one family walking slowly and sorrowfully to the ghetto, accompanied by gendarmes.

Non-Jews lined the streets watching in silence. No one said a word. No one said hello. Or goodbye. They stood soundlessly watching. Perhaps in their hearts they cheered that, at last, the Jews, enemies of the people, were being taken to the ghetto.

A relative received us in the ghetto. The four of us: Tateh, Mameh, Sheindy and I, huddled in a corner of the apartment, which was packed with children, the elderly, and ill people.

Our return to the ghetto was met with despondency by fellow Jews. "A bad sign," they muttered. "Things are going downhill and now there's no chance the law will alter in our favor." Several days after our arrival, rumors from the grapevine said that on the coming Friday there'd be another 'transport.' The word itself made people shudder. It had been recently clarified that 'transport' meant deportation to an unknown fate. No one knew the destination of these transports. We only knew that no one had come back.

One week after we arrived, another deportation was organized. Once again it was a Friday, a day on which we normally prepared for the approaching Sabbath: on June 3, 1944 a large group of Jews was led to the city's train station, including us. It was the last 'transport' from our area.

THE FINAL JOURNEY

Led like criminals down the city's main road, we still had no idea of our fate. We had no notion that we'd been sentenced to death. Lining the streets were non-Jews who had been friends, acquaintances, and school mates.

We had no idea where we were headed, and had only been told that we were being taken to labor camps. Once again there was a long procession: women carrying infants, old people, children, all with bundles slung over their backs. Children cried. The elderly prayed.

The column of people moved forward slowly. Germans hurried us along using whips. We walked along what seemed to be a never-ending road, aiding the elderly, supporting the ill, giving an arm to pregnant women. And that's how we were banished from our city and homes.

At the station we saw cattle cars hitched to a train, but who could have imagined that they were meant for us? Nor did we know at the time that this had been designated our final journey with our parents, traveling a one-way trip with no planned return.

Hungary's Jews believed they were protected and would not be harmed. What an illusion! We were taken to Auschwitz.

Through slits on the cattle car's sides I had one last peek at my home town. I was leaving everything I've ever know behind: my city, my past, without knowing what the future held nor how long we'd be on this journey. A long hoot sounded: loading the human cargo was complete.

As soon as the train began moving, all hell broke loose. It was so jam-packed that there was nowhere to sit; people fought over every millimeter of space. Our misery grew: unbearable heat; elderly pushed up against air vents, trying to get a breath of fresh air; the window couldn't be opened because it was covered by bars; nor we were permitted to push our hands out through the bars or throw anything out.

Night fell. Despite the darkness, it was impossible to sleep in the carriage. People would nod off for a few moments. We were completely disconnected from reality and the outside world. An infant cried. His embarrassed mother, with no alternative, opened her dress and put him to the breast. Glancing around, her eyes asked forgiveness from others because, in our world, a woman would never expose herself this way.

The train rolled on. The only sound was the engine's whistle and wheels clacking on the tracks. Morning light eventually seeped in through the small aperture. Someone shouted, "water!" A pregnant woman had fainted, but our water supply was diminishing. People banged on the carriage walls, screaming for help to no avail. Like a ghost train, the journey continued without interruption.

That day passed. So did another night. The water had run out. People's strength was visibly waning. In this packed carriage there was no toilet. A long hoot pierced the air. The train halted, tossing people from side to side and against each other. Peering through the small slits, my uncle saw the station sign: Katowice. We had reached Poland. A large number of people were gathered on the platform. My uncle asked one where our train was taking us; the man raised his hand and ran his index finger across his throat. To our slaughter. My uncle went ashen, trembling. "The Germans are taking us to our death!"

Everyone was attempting to access the door, trying to break it open and escape. People lost their minds, certain that their end was near. Of course, the doors were never opened. Shortly afterwards, the train moved on. Actually, it sped on, quickly leaving villages behind us. This hell in the carriage lasted for three days and three nights, with no water and no fresh air until, at last, the horrific journey came to an end.

AUSCHWITZ

We arrived at the Auschwitz death camps. The elderly were on the verge of collapse, the children bawled, fathers worried, and many fell ill along the way, needing help. After so much travel without food or drink, my head spun. I lost my balance and could barely stand up. Again the train pulled up sharply, throwing people, now too weak to stand firmly, onto each other. Peering through the small aperture, Tateh noticed nothing but very long rows of barracks.

Mameh had made sure we each had a suitcase packed with personal items. Tateh glanced down at my feet. "Change out of your pretty shoes and put on the winter ones. We've come to a wilderness." I really didn't want to do that, but I didn't want to oppose my father either. Quickly I pulled the high boots out and put them on. These ankle boots, packed at home before we left in the middle of summer, served me well in the camp. With me until liberation, they saved my life.

Tateh asked me to watch out for my younger sister, Sheindy. It was as though he felt that our ways would part. He repeated this several times. It was the last thing Tateh said to me, and impressed itself in my mind as his last will and testament.

The carriage doors opened. Strong light from outside blinded us. A large number of SS officers shouted orders, growling Dobermans on leashes by their sides. Prisoners in striped clothes boarded the carriage. Tateh asked where we were: "Death camps," they answered. "Here's where they kill and cremate the elderly and only the young stay alive." The prisoners' heads were shaven, they were extremely thin and frightened.

We tried to take a suitcase or even a small package with us, but the German guards facing us with their dogs screeched to leave them in the carriage. That's where we left our family photos, our past, our memories. The men in striped clothing dashed about, carrying out orders, not talking, while the SS shouted: "Schnell! Schnell! Disembark, Schnell!"

I wouldn't have separated from my parents so quickly had I known I'd never see them again. I thought this was just a temporary separation, that we'd be back together again as a family soon.

We were ordered to stand in lines. A quick hug, another quick kiss to our parents. Another kind word from Mameh, another concerned glance from Tateh. The pain of separation was fierce. The family had been torn apart. Now it was each to his or her own. Floodlights beamed down on us full force. It all happened so fast. We were in shock and confused, and extremely fearful.

Anyone not obeying the Germans' orders was set upon by a Doberman and whipped, or beaten with clubs. The sound of clubbing came from everywhere at once. Orders were given about which line to join: elderly men, elderly women, young males, young females, and even children, who were told they'll be joining their parents soon. When a child insisted on staying with her or his mother, the two weren't separated. Both were sent right away to the crematorium.

Sheindy stood next to me crying, trembling in fear, when suddenly she broke rank and ran towards Mameh. With some internal intuition Mameh sensed that Sheindy joining her would put her at risk and angrily shooed her back. "Go back to your sister Hilda. She'll look after you." Sheindy obeyed. Mameh had saved her from the cruel fate of immediate incineration.

My knees almost buckled from fear when Sheindy began

making her way towards Mameh. Now she stood next to me once more. Mameh wiped her tears. A woman who had given birth to seven children now stood in her row completely on her own.

The Germans shouted at us to move forward, but our beseeching eyes were focused on our parents, who we watched until they disappeared from view. An SS officer approached our row, whip in hand, Doberman at his side, and we set off at a march: "Links, rechts, links, rechts." We never saw our parents again after that. They were taken straight to the furnaces.

In this terrible place, each person was left to her or his own fate, for better or worse, without any help or guidance from parents or siblings.

A tall SS officer stood in front of us, signaling with a flick of one finger who should go left, who to the right. To life or to death. Later we learned the man's name: Dr. Mengele.

The elderly and ill were sent to be burned. Younger people, having successfully passed Mengele's discernment, walked through the Auschwitz entrance, the metalwork motto above the gate pronouncing: 'Arbeit Macht Frei.' Work will set you free.

Auschwitz-Birkenau was surrounded by electrified barbed wire fencing and tall watch towers. Entering the camp, we noticed row upon row of windowless sheds. We were made to sit on the ground in the area between them. Hour after hour we sat there waiting, no food, no water, nothing but the open sky above us. German guards made sure no one tried to escape. Young women who looked very odd to us, with shaven heads and wearing gray dresses and wooden clogs, approached and said that they were also Jewish prisoners from one of the previous transports to Auschwitz. They were already considered 'veterans' of this place. I remember thinking that if my sister had stood in front of me in a dress like that, her hair shaven, I'd have had a hard time recognizing her.

We, the newcomers, were still in our own civilian clothes and with full heads of hair. These veterans crowded around us. They wanted to hear news from the outside world, whereas we wanted to know about life in the concentration camp.

Auschwitz-Birkenau was right next to the crematorium, the young women explained. Smoke rising from the chimneys could be seen easily. That's where the elderly, children and the ill are taken. The strange odor we smell comes from bodies being burned. In those brief sentences they introduced us to camp life. I felt paralyzed, unable to believe what I'd heard. At that moment I was sorry I'd been born. I was sorry I'd been brought into this world. My entire world was instantly destroyed.

Later, after hours of waiting, SS officers arrived and began sorting us. A terrible fear filled me: what if my sister and I get separated? I was afraid that if they took her from me I'd never see her again. What should I do? Where could I hide her? After all, I'd promised Tateh that I'd look after her, but now the Germans were coming closer, not skipping anyone with their selection process.

My cousin Mali dropped a few years off her age. Getting the idea, I added two to mine, making myself eighteen. I told Sheindy to add two years, making her fifteen, but her appearance didn't match the number. The Germans were checking, choosing, separating girls aged thirteen and fourteen.

And now they'd reached us. The tall German, Mengele, as we'd later learn, raised his finger and pointed to Sheindy. "No!" I screamed, "I'm not letting her go, I don't want us to be separated, don't take her," I shouted. I hugged her tightly to me, but the Germans had no emotions, no sentiment. I was whipped once, twice, three times. My arms bent, my head spun, and I fainted, falling to the ground. The Germans pulled my thirteen year old sister Sheindy from my grasp. When I eventually came to, I was told that she'd been taken. No one knew where, nor whom to ask. Even if anyone did know, or thought they knew, they weren't about to say. I could only think of the worst possible option.

Returning to us, the Germans led us to the shower block where we left our clothes and our jewelry, but I had a hard time leaving my shoes behind and took them with me. After all, hadn't Tateh asked me to wear them? Before entering the shower, the German guard asked me to throw the shoes aside but I refused, and of course the whip came down on my back. I started running, the guard running after me. I went into the shower stall, which was already full of young women, getting as far from the door as possible until the German lost sight of me. He couldn't tell me apart from the other girls. He stood in the doorway for a few moments, then disappeared.

When we showered, German soldiers stood there watching our naked bodies, laughing at us. What terrible humiliation.

Leaving the shower block via a second door, we each received that gray dress and a pair of Dutch clogs. I put my own shoes back on and slept in them most of the time, fearing that if I ever removed them at night, I wouldn't find them in the morning. I guarded them like a precious treasure. These ankle boots served me well throughout the entire period I was in the concentration camp, until after our liberation, and I merit my father's advice with saving my life.

I remembered the veteran prisoners telling us to keep a close watch on our shoes because "shoes are your life." Many girls ended up with no shoes at all, the stocks having run out. Some tossed their clogs away because they caused rub wounds and painful blisters. Not a good move, because the ground was moist and muddy. Going barefoot brought you faster and much closer to death.

Things were moving fast. There was no time to think. Once again, we were standing in lines while young women brandishing scissors chopped our hair off. Many of our us, the new batch of women in the camp, began screaming, trying to open the doors and leave. Instantly the guards went into action, whipping everyone they could, trying to instill order, but the girls were hysterical by now. Nothing helped, of course. Our long hair was first cut short, then our heads were shaven. Friends couldn't recognize each other, sisters couldn't find each other, shaven heads had altered our appearances so drastically. From the veterans doing this job, we learned that Auschwitz-Birkenau was an extermination camp and every day that we remained alive was a miracle.

"Everyone's time comes," they said, "there's only one way out of this camp. Through the chimney." I hear what they're saying but cannot believe they aren't exaggerating.

In that hellhole, my soul breaking from sorrow over my sister being taken from me, I met a girl from our neighborhood, a classmate by the name of Rivka Yunger. She placed a cup of water to my lips and gently encouraged me, "Drink, it'll help you recover." Rivka, it turned out, had come to Auschwitz on the transport before mine and was already a veteran. She worked in the kitchen and was able to get a bucket of water out to help us, the new arrivals. Hearing word that a young woman had fainted, she quickly went in search of her, bringing a glass of water. Chance encounters of kindness like that could also be found in a death camp.

We were taken to a large field and told to sit down. We suffered from hunger and thirst but we were not permitted to ask, or even speak. So we sat on the ground for hours until food was brought: a single bowl of soup for ten of us! It was hard to guess what the soup was actually made from: the liquid was murky and a few vegetable peels floated in it. We drank it, dreaming of foods from home, the wonderful cooking and flavors our mothers produced. We asked the veteran prisoners again about the fate of our parents, of our families and, once again, were given the exact same answers, with slight variations to the words used.

When darkness fell we were taken to sleeping quarters. What a shock when we were directed into the toilet block! It was long, wide, with windows, and some thousand toilet seats arranged in long rows. We were horrified. Is this where we would spend the night? But, as always in Auschwitz, no questions can be asked. Each of us had to find somewhere to sit. Some of us sat on the toilets, others on the floor. I sat beneath an open window. It was hot and humid in the shed, and the mix of body odor and sweat almost choked us. Outside a driving rain fell: the fresh air coming through the window was a blessing.

The woman in charge of this shed entered, accompanied by her assistants, all carrying buckets filled with water. Every group of five of us received one cup of water. What a blessing. When the water distribution was complete, I got lucky: the cup remained with me. Rain flowed down from the shed's roof, large drops falling on the window. I drew as close as possible, holding my hand out, the cup hidden behind my back, collecting drips. At least that way I could moisten my dry lips.

But the guard standing outside saw what I was doing. He snuck up quietly and snatched the cup from my hand, then stood in front of the window and roared with rage. "You are prohibited from stealing rain! Make do with what you're given." *So this is Auschwitz*, I remember thinking, *a different world with different rules, and woe to any who don't stick to them.*

That night we slept sitting on the floor in the toilet block. We were terribly overcrowded. Standing up wasn't allowed, nor speaking or moving. With the windows closed, the heat became unbearable.

In the early afternoon we were moved to the living quarters, where bunks were set up three levels high along the shed's full length. Every bed held ten women. None was equipped with a mattress. One blanket was allocated to each ten of us. The block held some 1,000 to 1,200 young women.

Lying on my bunk in Auschwitz, I remembered something that happened to me at home when I was in the kindergarten adjacent to Tateh's shop. When kindergarten had ended one day, I left together with a group of children, but was so busy chatting that I never noticed where we were going and took the opposite direction. Children went back to their homes and I found myself alone in an unfamiliar environment. I walked on and on until I'd walked right out of the city.

Panicked and very afraid, I went over to a tree on the roadside, hugged it tight, and burst into tears. A man standing in his garden nearby heard me and came over, asked my name, where I was from, what my father did and, between one sob and another, I answered. He sat me on his bike and brought me back. This kind man also bought me cherries in a bag, which made me instantly stop crying. I ate hungrily. It turned out later that the man had no children, and he'd thought that if we couldn't find my parents, he'd adopt me.

When we reached the city, people he knew asked who the little girl on the bike was. He answered that he'd found me on the roadside, and asked if anyone knew my parents. He rode down several streets, checking with passersby, but no one had any idea. Eventually we went into the shop of one of my parents' friends, who knew exactly to whom I belonged. The man, whose name I can no longer remember, took me to our shop. As soon as the door opened, I leapt into Tateh's open arms. He held me close, and I wept and laughed at the same time. Afterwards, whenever that man would come into the city, he'd visit Tateh's store to ask after 'his' little girl.

***

At night we were locked in, no one coming or going until the morning. My second night without Mameh, without family, alone, somewhere in the Auschwitz hellhole.

Whispering among ourselves, we spoke of home, still unable to believe that we weren't with our parents and families, that our lives had collapsed, had been destroyed. As we lay on the wooden bunks at night after lights out following a wildly

33

emotional day, we promised each other that whoever lived would tell the world of these camp experiences.

Silence slowly fell, young women dreamt, some muttered in their sleep, one called out her husband's name, another the name of her son. Many dozed, woke, and whimpered.

Suddenly a loud ring was heard, the lights went on, and orders were given. "Raus! Raus! Alle zum Appell!" Out, out, everyone to roll call. Clubs came down on heads, screams bellowed from the unfortunate women who'd been hit. The woman in charge of the block and her assistants dashed about as though consumed by fire. We sprung from the bunks and literally ran outside.

For roll call we were ordered to stand in fives, without moving. Not a word came from our lips, we were so afraid. It was cold and I had on only a thin dress. Or perhaps it was my heart that felt cold? Someone fainted. We were forbidden from helping her up or even touching her in any way.

Roll call's silence was absolute, as though all 1,000 young women from our block had swallowed their tongues. The lives and deaths of these young women were in the cruel hands of the Blockältester, a female prisoner appointed by the SS to be in charge of the block. She doled out orders, teaching the newcomers how to behave in roll call.

First she said, "Stand in rows. Five to a row."

Then, "Stand in a straight line."

"Stand up, look ahead."

"Understood?"

No one said a thing.

We stood for hours at roll call until several German officers appeared, checked the number of women standing, and whether it matched the numbers they have. We were free to break the rows. Our third night in Birkenau.

Once again we're woken with shouts. Lights go on. Whips crack. Again the order, "Raus! Raus!" for roll call. A large number of SS officers enter the block, ordering us out as fast as possible.

After we're counted, we're given food: one slice of bread spread with a touch of margarine and jam. Dobermans and soldiers surround us. We wait for the next orders.

Where are we being taken in the middle of the night? Where are they sending us? No answers come to our unvoiced questions. Eventually the order is given, and we begin to march. I pray to God. *Guard and protect us. We're lost. We're abandoned.*

A fair distance later, we reach a large structure with tall chimneys through which tongues of flame erupt. Has our fate been cast? Are we going to be incinerated? A stench overwhelms us: burning bodies. We try scattering, moving away, but the soldiers with their barking Dobermans collect us immediately. Is this the end of the road for us?

We pass the crematoria's electrified fence. We are extremely scared. My hand had been gripping my slice of bread but, out of sheer fright, I must have dropped it without even noticing. What a pity. Even the guards are having a hard time controlling the young women's cries. My whole body is trembling. My legs don't want to obey me, and I barely take one step after the next, the tension and terror are so encompassing. Where are we being taken under cover of night's darkness?

Suddenly we change direction, distancing from the fence. A short while later, the furnaces are well behind us.

Dawn colors the sky. We've reached a train station, carriages ready and waiting for us. A weight is lifted from our hearts; we sigh with relief. This time, we're saved. We settle into the cattle cars, exhausted from the nightmare we've just been through. Although we're traveling to an unknown destination, at least we're still alive. That's how we left the Auschwitz hell. In my thoughts I bid the electrified barbed wire fence and the machine guns peeking from the watch towers goodbye. We're distancing ourselves from the furnaces and the stench of burning human flesh.

***

Sitting in the cattle car, I remember a story from home. One of my aunts lived in a village called Chomut (Chomutov) not far from Sevluš. I convinced Mameh that during the long summer vacation I should be allowed to travel to my aunt on my own and stay with her for a few days. Mameh said that I was still too young to travel alone, but I wouldn't give up. Eventually she agreed.

The great day arrived, Mameh packed a small valise for me and, excitedly, I said goodbye to the family. I sat on the wagon next to my uncle. He cracked the whip and the horse set off at a trot. I was thrilled, feeling like such a grownup although, at the time, I must've been no more than about seven. My aunt received me warmly. Her children invited me to join them for a walk to show me around.

The next morning my aunt had an announcement to make. "Today is laundry day and we're all going down to the stream to wash our clothes." Everything was collected in a large sheet, its ends tied, and the bundle thrown over a shoulder. The stream was perhaps some twenty minutes' walk from the house. My aunt moistened the items in the stream, soaped them one by one, placed them on a large rock and, using a wooden carpet beater, began slamming it against the laundry. She did this process twice: soaping, beating. Then she rinsed each item out carefully. Once she was finished, we put everything in large enamel bowls and headed back home.

The trouble began after night fell. I told my aunt that it had been a wonderful day, but now I wanted to go back home to sleep. My aunt said that was impossible and I could only return the next day. I couldn't wait for the night to be over. First thing the next morning, as dawn broke, my aunt sat me on the wagon and sent me back. The second I stepped into our yard, I burst into tears. Mameh and Tateh asked me why I was crying. I remember telling them it was nothing, something got into my eye but it's alright now. But Tateh knew that I was crying because I missed home, which was also why I returned so quickly.

KRAKÓW-PŁASZÓW

We traveled for several hours, eventually reaching the Kraków-Płaszów concentration camp. Barbed wire fences surrounded the place. *Auschwitz 2*, I was thinking. *No trees, no flowers, no birds. Nothing but Dobermans and their hungry stare, threatening to jump on us and shred us into pieces.* People here looked starved, fatigued and scared.

I was sent to work paving the internal Płaszów camp road. In charge of us was a Ukrainian SS guard, particularly tough and cruel, who whipped us to make us work faster. Rain poured down without pause. In nothing but my thin dress, I was soaked to the bone, but the job had to be done and better sooner than later. Ten of us worked in a line. Next to me was a woman who couldn't maintain the murderous pace set by the guard so, every few minutes, I moved to her row and helped her advance to make sure she was in line with the rest of us.

But the guard noticed. He started shouting, enraged. "Don't you know you're forbidden to help?" He ran to me, extremely angry, and whipped my back five times. I was on the verge of collapse, but crying is forbidden, and showing pain is forbidden. Work must go on. The job must get done.

Once the day had ended we went back to the camp. Despite my bloodied back I kept the screams of agony inside. It was difficult to sit, more so to lie down.

I spent the night prone on the floor because I was unable to climb into my allocated third-level bunk. The next day work continued. We were paving on a hill, the other side of which was very steep. My back ached so much that I couldn't straighten up. I needed to think of a solution. I knew I had to find a way to get out of working. That kept my mind busy.

A crazy idea suddenly came to mind and I acted fast. I stood on the slope's edge and acted as though I was fainting and losing my balance. I fell and rolled down the slope to the bottom, about some twenty meters. That's where a different group of women worked moving stones from one place to another. As I rolled down I could feel not only every small stone but every slight bump in the ground searing the wounds on my back. Worst of all, a branch caught on the fabric of my dress, adding fresh wounds.

Pretending to be unconscious, I opened my eyes just a smidgen. I could see women coming over to me. They checked and, after seeing I was still breathing, one grabbed my shoulders, another my legs, and dragged me to their block not far away. When they picked me up pain tore through the open wounds. I tried moistening my parched lips in the rain, which still hadn't stopped. The women brought some of their meager soup in a tin container to my lips. Drop by drop I drank, restoring a fraction of my strength. I lay there until the workday was over, returning to camp with everyone.

Back in Kraków-Płaszów, I couldn't believe my eyes: the camp had been set up inside a Jewish cemetery! Chunks of broken tombstones were scattered everywhere, the names of the deceased still clearly visible. The stones had been used for various purposes such as paving paths and camp access routes. The thought of leaving our block every morning, going outside for roll call, and finding myself in a cemetery was sickening.

Meanwhile I'd been transferred to the quarry's night shift. After breaking up rocks into large chunks, we had to collect them all and bring them to the carts. It usually required two or three of us to carry these boulders. Carts, which stood waiting on iron tracks, were pushed along by six women. Often we lacked the strength to restrain and control them, and they'd go flying down, rock fragments scattering everywhere.

Work never ceased in Płaszów's two quarries which kept female prisoners working in two shifts, day and night. One day after filling a cart and pushing it along its track, a woman from our group fainted. The officer standing nearby saw her fall, pulled out his pistol, and shot her. We were so scared that we continued working with renewed strength. My knees shook. I didn't dare look back. Guards kept shouting to work faster. We obeyed. We simply wanted to stay alive.

On another occasion I saw a dog rip a woman's flesh because she dared empty her bladder during work time. Engrossed in thoughts about what I'd witnessed and the threat of the whip on my back got me working again full pelt.

A number of Jews in Poland managed to hide but, if discovered, they were brought to the camp, shot once, and thrown into the furnaces while still hovering between life and death. The stench of burning flesh stained the entire camp's air. Of all my war memories, what I experienced in Kraków-Płaszów is engraved in my mind as the worst of all.

The train to Auschwitz concentration camp, 'Konzentrationslager' in German, reached the Płaszów camp's gates. We were taken direct from our living quarters and stuffed into a shed where guards closed and locked the doors. I lay down to rest a little on a bunk. Events followed each other at a crazy pace. Mere hours ago I'd left Auschwitz! I badly wanted to close my eyes, perhaps sleep a little, but the doors were thrown open harshly. A guard entered. "Raus! Raus!"

Like everyone else, I ran out for roll call. Suddenly I saw a group of children, row upon row of them standing in fives, sorrowful, starving, their huge eyes gazing questioningly as they waited for orders. It was wonderful, in a way, to hear the sound of children again, but several days later they disappeared; they had been taken to Auschwitz. I did not ask what happened to them.

Food at Płaszów was a miserable affair. Breakfast was a cup of murky water presented as coffee, accompanied by one slice of bread with something cooked into it that was meant to stop women from menstruating. Lunch was vegetable soup with not a vegetable in sight, only potato peels. The worst of the soups was lentil soup, of a disgusting yellow hue and an even more disgusting taste. For a period of time we were given lentil soup twice a day, at lunch and dinner, and I had such trouble ingesting it. I'd take a spoonful, close my eyes, and try to make myself swallow it. But after several spoons I couldn't continue, and simply left it in the bowl, which was incomprehensible in camps in general and in Płaszów in particular. Others tried convincing me that if I refused to eat I'd end up starving and looking like a *Muselmann*, literally Muslim in German, indicating the inability to stand due to a combination of exhaustion and starvation-induced muscular atrophy in their legs, but used cynically to describe walking skeletons. Nothing helped. I couldn't swallow the soup.

Throughout my marriage those yellow lentils never came into my kitchen!

The only so-called good thing at the Płaszów concentration camp was hot water. In one of the showers, hot water flowed round the clock. I could never fathom how we were provided this luxury. We'd go in groups to the shower, only after requesting permission. Trying to take advantage of this hot water, I'd get away whenever possible to drink some. I thought of it as a replacement for tea or coffee, and even as a substitute for the insufferable soup, drinking three or four full cups in one go.

I always felt that the hot water saved my life, in some measure. In all the camps I was sent to, I tried to maintain body cleanliness as much as I could, and did the same in Płaszów; however, it didn't help much because everyone there was infected by lice.

One day we were informed at roll call that we were leaving Kraków-Płaszów. I was pleased. Although we had no idea where we were going, there was always some hope that, in the next camp, things would be even a fraction better. Thoughts about escaping never left my mind, but I needed an appropriate opportunity. I didn't have a consolidated plan, but I knew that any slip-up with an attempt to escape would mean death on the spot.

***

Six months before we were expelled from our homes, I woke panicked from a frightening dream. My mother came to me right away, attempting to reassure me. She asked what I'd dreamt, and I described it in detail. I was sitting among sheaves of hay in the field. They were organized next to one another in a row. One side of a sheaf was open and inside was an empty space. Driving rain came down and lightning lit the field as though it was daytime! Furiously loud thunder rolled above my head. It felt like the end of the world. I tried burrowing deep into the sheaves, hoping to find shelter from the rain. Suddenly a bee appeared, circled me several times, and began to hover as though intending to sting me.

I was so scared of being bitten, I tried shooing the bee away. It distanced, and then approached again. Then I heard a voice coming from the sky. A deep, strong voice called out. "Don't be afraid. The bee won't sting you. The bee will be with you and look after you wherever you go."

My mother was amazed. She decided to consult with the rabbi, seeking an interpretation for these odd images. Back home again, she told my father what the rabbi had said, not noticing that I wasn't far away and could overhear. The rabbi had said I was deeply privileged to dream such a scenario, that the dream was a caution against the coming destruction, that I would be in great danger, and would need to cope with many difficulties in order to remain alive. But he assured my mother that I would indeed manage, and get through the harsh times to come with great valor.

When I asked my mother what the rabbi had explained, she didn't want to answer, saying only that I was too young to understand the dream's meaning. She promised that, when I was older, she'd tell me. I viewed the rabbi as sage, and treated whatever he said with the utmost respect. Later, after we were banished from our homes and while I was in the death camps, I remembered the dream. In the harshest of times it propped up my spirits and I'd repeat the rabbi's words about experiencing difficult times and bravely getting through them. His interpretation gave me the strength to keep going.

FROM KRAKÓW-PŁASZÓW
BACK TO AUSCHWITZ

The train and its load of prisoners sped back to Auschwitz-Birkenau. New rules. New protocols. The same barbed wire fence. The same watch towers. The same furnaces, their chimneys visible wherever you looked. Back through the same arched gateway to Birkenau and it's deceitful slogan, '*Arbeit Macht Frei.*'

We were led to the showers, disinfected and, again, our hair was cut and our heads then shaved. At the shower block we were ordered to discard the clothes given to us at Kraków and were given clean clothing. That's how we got rid of the lice. Once again I was able to hold on to my shoes. Admittedly my back tasted the whip for doing so, but it was completely worth it.

How can I collect my life's fragments? How can I make such sharp turns and, within hours, forget-slash-erase everything, repeatedly starting over? At night I wept. In the morning I emanated confidence, drawing on the remnants of my strength, telling myself I had to keep going, I had to start the day by putting my right foot forward, I had to hope for the best, even though we were accompanied by SS officers. We walked to our barracks. Everything replayed: bunks three levels high lining both sides of the barracks, and the broad wooden bases. The same block, sans windows. The same sensations of disconnect from the outside world.

Hearing the Kapo's whistle, we bounded out of bed and, in fear, dashed to the yard and quickly aligned in fives, ready for roll call. It was 4 a.m. and icy cold. All we had on were flimsy dresses of the thinnest cloth. The cold penetrated every part of our body and soul. Like sculptures, we stood motionless, losing our sense of time. Sometimes we stood for two or three hours until the SS officer came to count us. Only after that we were allowed to go.

Not everyone in Auschwitz-Birkenau worked. Instead, we had roll calls held four or five times a day but, in a way, they were worse than work. If any of the young women didn't stand up straight or moved in the slightest, overcome with the fatigue of standing for so long, or if one of us wanted to help another who fainted, we'd be doled out a collective punishment: standing with our arms raised for hour upon hour.

One morning I went into the yard, taking up a position next to the electrified fence to talk to other young women from the neighboring concentration camp. We'd shout out names of family members, friends and neighbors in the hope that some were still alive. One day I shouted my sister Sheindy's name: could she be on the other side of this fence? I didn't believe it possible, but I shouted anyway. Suddenly a voice answered! "Are you looking for your sister Sheindy? She's in Barrack One with me!"

Unbelievable!

I found my sister Sheindy!

In all this chaos, in this Gehenna, this hell, I found her in the adjacent camp on the other side of this fence!

The girl who answered me offered to call Sheindy right away. Some minutes later there she stood, trembling, weeping. My little sister was in the children's section, Camp 6. I was in Camp 8. The electrified fence separating us, preventing us from getting closer. The noise was tremendous: girls and women incessantly shouting names.

On either side of the fence was a section of ground that we

were not permitted to approach. We needed to shout incredibly loudly in order to hear each other. But we could hardly speak, we were so emotional. We could only weep, and weep more. What a sad, heart-rending encounter.

I learned that Sheindy was in the camp where Mengele conducted weekly selections, deciding who would live and who would die. My sister was lucky: his reach had yet to call on her group.

Every day after roll call we raced to the fence to share our experiences, remembering incidents from home, reminiscing about the family, wondering who of our siblings was still alive.

After the guards shooed us away from the fence, we would sit on the ground or walk around the camp, waiting tensely for the next encounter. One day we received an order to line up. German women sat at tables and wrote numbers on the young women's arms. I held my arm out, like the others, and was labeled 4-22533. This deeply upset me, so I raced to the taps to wash the number off. It didn't, of course. The tattoo's ink remained bright and clear, as it has to this day.

"From now on," we were told, "you will forget your names." That's how the Nazis snatched from me the last thing I still had with me from home: my name.

One day I tried sharing my daily portion of bread with my sister. Early in the morning before roll call, I hid half of it under the blanket but, when I returned, it was gone. One of the veterans explained. "Here in Birkenau you never try to keep bread. If you've got some, eat it. if you don't eat it right away, you'll end up hungry. Remember my words."

In Auschwitz, the pot of soup was customarily hauled from the kitchen to the distribution point by two young women. Frequently prisoners would run to the pot before they even began doling it out, dipping their cups or bowls in before scattering off.

One day my cousin convinced me to do that too, dip my cup in so that we'd benefit from an extra portion. I followed her suggestion but, just then, an SS officer showed up and saw me. He ordered me to stop, but I raced off at top speed around the blocks with him hot on my heels. He wanted me to throw the cup away but, in Auschwitz, a cup meant life because, without it, there was no way to eat. So we ran past the first block, the second, and then the third. Eventually he stopped, perhaps having tired or gotten fed up. I slipped into a group of young women. Most of the soup had sloshed out by then, but at least I still had the cup. I was furious with my cousin, and never tried that trick again.

At night on the exposed wooden bunk after lights out, I cried, longing for home, family, my peaceful life of not so long ago. The thought that my parents had suffered a bitter fate kept me from sleeping properly. I hadn't heard from them, or about them, and rumors persisting that they'd long since been taken to the crematoria turned out to be true, a fact I could not accept.

In my imagination I saw them standing, in almost their last moments, in the shower blocks, naked, poisonous gas flowing from ceiling vents and killing them. They hadn't even had an opportunity to bid their children goodbye. It was too terrible to think about.

Another new place, another unknown destination: one day we were informed that we were being taken to a labor camp. I wanted to tell my sister. How could I possibly leave her now? Who knew when we'd see each other again? My heart was broken: I couldn't hug or kiss her, only wave countless times, my sister on her camp's side of the fence, me on mine, and no more than a few meters separating us.

I heard the order to stand for roll call. One last quick wave, one last kiss blown, and I ran to my spot in my row of five.

Tears in my eyes, my heart clenched, I left Sheindy behind the fence in Auschwitz, awaiting her fate at Mengele's whim.

LEAVING AUSCHWITZ-BIRKENAU

We were loaded onto a freight truck, each of us receiving a portion of bread for the journey. We clutched it close and nibbled slowly until it was gone.

About two days later we reached a forest, the name of which I don't remember. And there we came upon a weapons factory entirely blanketed in snow – our new workplace. It truly felt as though we'd been brought to this isolated location to die.

Snow kept falling, the cold chilled our bones, and we hunkered down in our threadbare clothes as best we could. We were brought into new blocks which appeared to have been freshly constructed. Once again the multi-level bunks without mattresses, and one blanket to each bunk. We wouldn't have dared ask about heating. The kitchen, still unfinished, was not yet outfitted with utensils, let alone food items.

Roll call. The SS officer informed us that since the kitchen was as yet unfinished, food would be brought to us from the city. Had I caught that correctly? Food would be brought from a city? In other words, we weren't in some distant forest where no one would have any inkling of our existence? Clearly we were not far from a populated area. For some reason that made me happy.

***

That night I tried conjuring up images of my parents, picturing us in the garden under our beloved apple tree. Seated round the table in its fixed place, we were biting into freshly harvested grapes.

**

Often I tried bringing my parents into my thoughts but it didn't always work. Had I already lost them forever? The idea left me deeply disappointed. Would I never embrace them again? I'm so young, and still need them!

But foremost thought, constantly whirring in my mind, was how to escape. "I can't hold out in a place like this," I told myself sorrowfully.

The next morning the SS officer at roll call spoke about the weapons factory where we'd be working, located some five kilometers from our residential block and accessed on foot, there and back.

While we stood there, another officer arrived, commanding women who know how to weave to take a step forward. Of course I knew nothing about weaving, but was so keen on getting away from this accursed place that I needed to make a snap decision: stay in the forest, or take one step forward. I took that step.

GREENBERG

It was my hunch that the whole weaving issue was nothing but a German ploy. Were they plotting to murder us in this snowy forest? I decided that I'd gamble on life or death. My heart pounded so hard that I was afraid I'd collapse. But I stepped forward, head held high. From the corner of my eye I saw my cousin also step forward, as did several others of us.

The SS officers did not interrogate us or even ask any questions. They signaled for us to climb into the trucks and, once again, we were heading to who-knew-where. Another new place. Another glimmer of hope that perhaps things there might be a little easier.

Slowly the forest was left far behind. Several hours of travel later, we approached a city which, judging by the sign, was called Greenberg. What a wonderful moment! We could see homes, trees, flowers, birds, shops, and people walking freely through the streets. Life! We could see life being lived. We were back in civilization, back among the living.

The trucks continued through the city, turned left, then right, left and right. We couldn't believe our good luck. Would we stay in the city? We became excited. We shared our thoughts.

Outside a large building, the trucks pulled up to a stop, gates were opened, and the trucks drove into a large courtyard. We breathed with relief. We're staying in the city. So far, so good!

The factory itself was underground, a huge well-organized building with central heating operating day and night. It contained a proper factory-style kitchen, rows of tables and benches set up in a dining hall. In the sleeping quarters we saw bunk beds, each with several blankets and, most importantly, mattresses! Incredible! Hallelujah!

We wandered about the large hall not believing our eyes. Had our fate suddenly improved so dramatically? Within a matter of hours?

I remember thinking that, if miracles exist, this must be one of them.

While we ate our hot lunch, the cook, also a Jewish prisoner, told us that hundreds of young women lived here but were currently at work. She reassured us that we had no reason to worry, that conditions here were reasonable, and we prisoners would be treated fairly humanely.

Was this a palace, I wondered? The heating warmed us; the cook's welcome encouraged us; we waited for the other prisoners to return. And they did, bringing noise, tumult, laughter, joking. They were warmly dressed and looked healthy. All had coats. Just as importantly, they all had hair, some cut short, some a little longer, but it was clear that their heads weren't shaven as in Auschwitz.

The young women came over to us, chatted, and received us warmly, explaining the house rules, adding that if we kept them, our lives here would be good. We were grateful to them.

In this camp, most of the SS officers were women who lived in a separate building nearby and didn't cause us much bother.

At evening roll call the *Aufseherin*, the female SS officer, told the Blockältester in charge of us that 999 Jewish prisoners would be present for dinner. That was how the Germans conveyed their messages. The Aufseherin also informed us that the next morning we would be taken to work in the weaving factory.

And that turned out to be no further than across the road. We set out from the gates of our sections and entered the factory's yard. We were not allowed to talk when crossing the road. The factory's gates clanged shut behind us, were locked, and armed guards kept watch. No one entered. No one left until the shift was over. But what joy! No need to walk kilometers each way in snow, rain and icy cold!

We soon understood that this was where the clothing brought by hundreds of thousands of Jews to the camps were delivered, to this factory. As the Jews arrived in Auschwitz, whatever they were wearing at the time was replaced by thin dresses or striped shirt-dresses and the confiscated clothing was bundled into massive bales and handed out to us as prisoners. The word 'Auschwitz' was clearly visible on each bale.

Every time I heard that word it made me tremble. A realization hit me: no matter where you were sent, Auschwitz came after you somehow. The factory I was now working in recycled the clothing, the final outcome being warm blankets for Wehrmacht soldiers, the unified armed forces of Nazi Germany.

Warehouses were stuffed with new blankets folded to perfection. How sad it made me to think that every folded blanket enfolded a Jewish family's tragedy. Initially I was tasked with sorting. We opened bales, shuddering at what we might find, and sorted the items: women's coats, men's suits, little girls' dresses, skirts, blouses. Every so often we'd find banknotes and other treasures sewn into shoulder pads or hems. Pockets gave up keys, photos, medicines. We removed buttons, unstitched seams, and transferred the items to the next department.

On one occasion, after opening a particularly large bale and beginning to remove the clothing, my eyes suddenly caught sight of a badge attached to a jacket's lapel. The badge looked so familiar. I started tugging at the jacket, pulling one sleeve free, then the next, and suddenly I was holding the jacket, stunned by disbelief. It was Tateh's! Acknowledged as a war-wounded from fighting in WWI, at the time referred to as The Great War, he'd received this badge as a mark of excellence in battle, and kept it pinned to the lapel.

I began shaking, so emotional that I was sure I'd pass out. I knew there was no way I could get this jacket out of the factory, yet I couldn't give it up. I would need to act quickly. That was the only option I could see. Cutting away at the lapel with scissors, I freed the badge, slipping it into my pocket.

Countless German citizens also worked in the factory in a so-called 'volunteer arrangement' for the sake of the homeland and the war. They were dispersed across the various departments, several in my department too. Most were in their fifties to sixties. A German woman working with me was watching closely. Seeing me begin to buckle, she quickly made me lie down on a pile of clothing and took care of me until I recovered. What a twist of fate!

These Germans had never heard of Auschwitz or the crematoria, had no idea why we were in Germany or what sort of crime we had committed that would bring us to this factory as prisoners. So I told them. I described the furnaces. I detailed how we were taken from our homes. I explained about ghettos and deportations, how we'd arrived at this factory, and that these clothes belonging to murdered Jews. But they didn't believe me. No matter how carefully or logically I presented the facts, they could not believe that what I said was possible. To them I had made up terrible stories about their countrymen.

Although the German civilian workers had received dire warnings by the SS, "not to fraternize with the prisoners," they were decent to us. Sometimes they'd bring us cake, apples or sandwiches, and sneak them to us when the SS weren't looking. What a paradox reality can be.

For several weeks I worked in the factory but had never seen any of the weaving machines. One day a group of prisoners, me among them, was chosen, and taken to a vast hall where hundreds of weaving machines stood. The instructor, a German citizen, took me over to one and taught me the art of weaving. He showed me how to tie the correct knots if threads tore, how to position the two little 'boats' that guided the threads in from both edges of the machine, and slowly I learned the profession. Once the supervisor saw that I could function independently, he went to teach another young woman, after reassuring me that if I encountered any problem, I should not hesitate to seek his help.

Not long afterwards, the instructor came over to say that, due to a shortage of workers, he has no choice but to have me work on two machines at once – one in front of me, and one behind my back. And he taught me how to do that, too.

One day while I was inserting the 'threader boats' and activating the machine, one boat came free and went flying at full force. The instructor, standing only meters from me, saw what was happening but never moved from his spot. The boat was heading towards him and passed about ten centimeters from his eye! Eventually it wedged into a pole. I was so scared that I couldn't speak and was sure I would faint.

The instructor signaled that I should follow him into the office because the noise in the work hall was deafening. Certain that the worst outcome possible awaited me, I followed, knowing that he could have been seriously injured, if not dead! The man was actually a German citizen, not an SS officer.

He asked me if I realized how dangerous the incident was, and all I could stutter was, "y..." barely at a whisper. He was quiet for a long time. I began to sweat profusely. Eventually he said that he wouldn't turn me in to his superiors, the SS, because if he complained about me they'd punish me severely, and that he would give some thought to a deserving punishment. I couldn't believe my ears.

Whatever the punishment he'd come up with couldn't possibly be as bad as what the SS would dole out. A while passed before the instructor transferred me to a different department. When I met him by chance one day in a different section, he said that he'd considered having me spend three days in solitary confinement but, after I'd been relocated, he decided to forget about the matter.

Solitary was a completely closed container positioned in the dining hall. It was the camp's prison. Inside was a bench on which the prisoner slept. Food was passed through bars, and everyone could view the prisoner. The instructor was a pleasant man, and my impression was that he pitied me. But I never forgot the incident and every time I inserted the leader boats into the machine, I double and triple checked that they were correctly lodged.

Among the Jewish prisoners working in the factory was a pregnant woman. Only in her second month, she underwent the concentration camp experience, then managed to get herself here because no one had noticed the pregnancy. We were all very tense about this. After the birth, would they let her keep the infant? Take it from her? Inform us at roll call that there were now one thousand prisoners, or continue to relate as though we were still only 999?

The big day came, the woman's labor pains began, and she was taken to the clinic. We stood there, huddled at the doorway, waiting. Several Aufseherin also hovered about, entering, exiting, their faces angry. Suddenly we heard a baby's cry. The nurse, a Jewish woman, came out to tell us it was a boy. "Mazal tov," she said, as we customarily do. Good fortune? Was this good fortune? That night at roll call the newborn was not numbered as one of us.

Greenberg camp was located in the city. From the windows of adjacent houses residents could see what was happening with us, just as we could peer in at our neighbors whose children would stand at the glass gazing at us, the prisoners.

Normal children, living in with their Mama and Papa in their family home.

Children whose parents looked after them, cared for them, got joy from them, tried to dispel their fears.

Children who went to school and, upon returning home, found their smiling Mama inside, the aromas of her cooking filling the home.

Children who went to sleep with a goodnight kiss and a good morning smile, for whom sandwiches were made and who were walked to their front gate where goodbyes were waved as the children walked to school.

How long it had been since I'd sat with my family at a table set for a meal? Months? Years? Perhaps a jubilee had passed! Everything was a blur, hard to recall, but also impossible to completely forget.

Once again my thoughts wandered back to my home.

***

One of our schoolteachers had been such a good soul. She always knew what was happening in the classroom, paying attention to each of us. Students felt safe about approaching her for advice on issues large and small. Often she would visit students at home to keep parents apprised regarding problems arising at school.

Every morning this teacher would enter the students' names in her diary. One day she noticed that a girl was missing. The teacher asked if we knew why. Another student who lived not far away said that her shoes had been taken for repair and she didn't have a second pair. It was winter, and snow had been falling non-stop. The teacher removed her boots and sent them home with the student's neighbor. Not long afterwards the student and the neighbor were back in class. The teacher spent the day shoeless at her desk but, when the school day was over, the student wearing the teacher's boots was accompanied home by her neighbor, who then returned the boots.

Two days after the birth we returned from work and heard heartbreaking cries. Two Aufseherin, the female SS guards, had taken the baby, leaving the mother sobbing. She cried for many days afterwards. We all did what we could to look after her until she recovered from the trauma.

We young women would make forays into the factory's clothing department and take items for ourselves, mending dresses, trying on blouses, or shortening skirts. You might have thought in the evenings that you were in a sewing workshop. Each of us had a small pile of clothing next to our beds.

We went to work in the gray clothes we'd been given but later, in our living quarters, changed out of them, dressing the way we wished. The Germans never interfered.

One day the Aufseherin told us that that we could each take a coat from the factory supply. How happy we were! We'd dreamed of having coats but never imagined the dream would come true. In a bundle of items, I found a checkered blanket of thin, beautifully made wool, and decided to take it out of the factory. I wrapped it around my body, held it in place by a length of string, and put my dress back on, praying that I'd get back to my room without being stopped. Yes! I was safely through the gates. The guard hadn't noticed I'd gotten a bit plumper.

The others helped me cut the blanket into a flowing skirt and a matching vest. Not having a sewing machine, we sat hand-stitching for hours. I also brought a matching blouse and pretty scarf out of the factory. One evening some of the young women, including me, decided to wear our new clothes to roll call. Suddenly I got very nervous, fearing that the guards would not view our actions kindly. It felt to me like tempting fate. I decided to go back to our room and change, avoiding unwarranted problems, but right then I heard the whistle. I had no choice but to stand in line for roll call.

Two Aufseherin had been signaled by the camp supervisor to begin. They started walking towards where we stood in fives, according to the rules.

The silence was deathly. No one moved. The Germans stared

at those of us in our different clothes. Facing us, they whispered between themselves. In my heart I knew I should never have forgotten where I was, even for an instant.

Unluckily for me, at that roll call I was in the front row. The time it took for the Aufseherin to consult with each other felt like an eternity. When they were done, they began counting us: five, ten, fifteen, twenty. Roll call was over. the Aufseherin left. I never wore those clothes again in the camp. The Jewish Blockäl-tester was called in to the SS office and was ordered to halt all sewing at night, and that ended that. It was of utmost importance, she told us right away, that we fulfill the factory's work quotas, that no complaints should be received by our superiors, and that the camp's cleanliness should be maintained at all times. Beyond that, they barely paid attention to what we did after work hours.

In retrospect, the clothes we took from the bales at the factory literally saved our lives, but more on that later.

One day when I was in Kraków-Płaszów, the Nazis stood us in a row, took a brush, dipped it into a bucket filled with red paint, and marked a stripe down the backs of our dresses from to bottom. In Auschwitz men were given a shirt and pants made of blue and gray striped cloth. Women wore gray cloth dresses. Our shaved heads were instant giveaways that we inmates of the concentration camp.

At Greenberg they found a different way to mark us. The coats we took were returned to the sewing workshop, a large 15 x 15 centimeter square was cut out of the back, and a patch made of striped material like that used in the concentration camp was inserted. The patch became our trademark should we dare try to escape.

During our stay at Greenberg, life was somewhat calmer. We were treated reasonably: we enjoyed fair amounts of food, appropriate clothing and a warm place to sleep. I repeated one prayer over and over: let me remain here until we're released.

Upon arriving at Greenberg I worked in the selection department and then in the weaving department. But the factory contained additional sections, including one where raw materials were repurposed. It looked like cotton-wool, but was soggy, and a good deal of effort was needed to repeatedly plunge the rake with its very long handle into this stuff in order to reach the room's four corners. This material was then collected from the floor by hand and transferred to the large aperture of a machine standing in the room's center and, from there, it went down wide pipes to the next department.

Work in the raw materials processing department was considered one of the factory's toughest jobs. At a certain roll call, the SS officer announced that anyone volunteering to work the night shift there would receive a double portion of food and a pair of pants. He explained that work there was in pairs: two young women per shift. We usually went to work in our dresses, but it was still cold. A pair of pants appealed to me and would greatly help me through the winter, as would the additional food. I volunteered immediately, together with another prisoner with whom I'd become friendly.

During one of our shifts we had been told to clear four rooms of this wet raw material. No Aufseherin was supervising; only an SS guard was in the vicinity, glancing in periodically to check that we were doing our job. It was hard work; we returned to camp exhausted, unable to straighten our backs, our entire bodies aching, but slowly we adapted to the manual labor.

This new job was monotonous and left us a lot of time to think. My thoughts always went back to my parents, murdered in Auschwitz, and my two sisters Goldie and Hannah who'd lived in Budapest at the time of our expulsion from home. I wondered if they were still in Budapest, and whether Frieda and my married sister, Rozie, her husband Zoli and their little boy Miki were alright. I also wondered what had happened to my brother, Zeril-Hersch. They'd all lived in Bratislava and had been taken to Auschwitz while we were still living at home but, since then, we'd heard no news about them. Our large, beautiful family, sent off to different locations: who could imagine where they were now?

One day we entered the factory and were surprised to discover that none of the German citizens had shown up. The sound of tanks, now heard very loudly in the city, had frightened them so much that they'd fled. Rumors were flying about that the Russian army was close to Silesia. Scared, the Germans decided to move further inland into Germany.

Indeed the sound of tanks approaching made us realize that our liberators were not far off. SS officers were on edge, which influenced their attitude towards us. Another rumor spread: the Germans were going to shut the factory and move us elsewhere. We began searching for warm clothing, each of us taking several items out of the factory on a daily basis, hiding the clothing under our dresses. At the least, we wanted to be sure we were outfitted with warm apparel if and when we'd need to leave the camp.

We were woken earlier than usual one morning. The noise of tanks was much closer. Suddenly all the SS officers gathered. We understood that an evacuation was about to take place. And it did, much faster than we'd guessed. The Nazis burned all the documents in the factory's offices as though the devil was chasing them down. The main thing was to leave no trace of the camp.

I had no idea when the war would end, but the noise of tanks coming ever closer, on one hand, and the Nazis' clear fear of the approaching Russian soldiers, on the other, raised my spirits.

EVACUATING GREENBERG

There we stood outside in roll call, in the dark. An SS officer notified us that we were leaving, and we should hurry
and ready ourselves for evacuation. The officer's instructions
were that we'd receive one portion of food for the journey, and
that taking bundles and packages with us was forbidden: we
could only leave with the clothes we wore. "That's an order!" he
said firmly.

At that point we had no idea that the journey would be long,
or that it would be on foot, walking us through snow and cold.
His announcement sent us spinning. Shouting, crying, and the
insufferable noise of tanks mixed with the nervous energy of
999 young women being taken elsewhere. Once again, to the
unknown.

I studied the pile of clothing I'd slowly built up and began
dressing. Shirts, sweaters, a vest, scarves, pajamas wound
around my legs. The pants I'd earned for having worked in the
raw materials department were a true blessing, covering the
other layers of clothing. It was important, I knew, to be protected from the cold. What a tragic-comic sight we were, making us
alternately cry and laugh when we looked at each other.

Our departure from Greenberg was anything but planned
in an organized fashion. Quite the opposite: it was panicked
and chaotic. The Germans decided to evacuate us in fear of the
Russians' growing closeness, but it didn't alter their attitudes
towards us: they still acted as though they were rulers of the

world. The Red Army's advance was catastrophic for Germany but, for us, it represented the buds of our redemption, and now we were once again being made to distance, turning liberation into far less of a reality.

With a shriek of the whistle, the last roll call in Greenberg was conducted and the door opened. In a rush, 999 young women exited the building. What a long, sorry and odd procession. The whistle again. Germans require order: we must straighten up our rows! So we stood in fives in front of the gate on a cold snowy morning with a portion of food in our hands, ready to move. SS officers and their dogs guarded us as though we were some unique treasure. Out we went, leaving the camp behind, only to discover that we'd be going wherever we're going on foot.

The march of death.

And it was evening, and it was morning, a new day.

We had no clue where we were headed but, in our wildest imagination we couldn't have conjured such a march – in winter, in the snow, in the cold. We walked through fields. We marched through villages whose residents stared at us as though we were apparitions. They asked where we came from and where we were going but we were forbidden from answering. They wanted to give us water but the soldiers guarding us urged us on by driving their Dobermans into action and by cracking whips above our heads. Anyone who'd broken rank to take something from townsfolk quickly ran back to the group, tears in their eyes, joining the line, marching on.

As we passed through the forests, the German guards murdered the weaker young women unable to keep walking. One gunshot, that's all it took. Here and there a young woman would lie down on the snow, utterly exhausted, saying it was enough, she had no strength to walk anymore, no strength to continue with this suffering. She wanted to die. The guards mercilessly fulfilled her wishes.

The entire time, I was planning how to escape. I came up with various scenarios for how to flee the death march, the dogs and the guards. Sharing my ideas with my cousin, she agreed to cooperate. Either we die in this accursed death march, I said, or we die trying to flee, but it's worth trying. On we marched, leaving nothing but deep footprints in the snow, and corpses. On we marched, having no idea of the destination or what the next day would bring.

Evening followed dusk, followed by night, and on we marched through open fields on a road lined on both sides by high, overgrown hedges. Would this be a good time to activate our plan? We could hide behind the bushes until everyone had passed, and then go in another direction... but where? We had no idea.

We broke away from our line and began running towards the hedges. But, what's this? All the young women in the rows behind us simply followed our lead! Because of the darkness they thought it was the right path! The guards sensed something wrong and immediately herded us back onto the road.

I wasn't giving up though and, a few seconds later, tried again. This time we did it! Hunkering down, we hid behind the hedge until the procession had passed, then began running without any idea where we were or where we were going.

For some twenty minutes we ran. We could hear the barking dogs. In the black of night we couldn't see anything but, by the sound's growing strength, I realized a dog was coming our way. My cousin kept running. I decided to lie down and play dead, holding my breath once the dog was next to me, sniffing around. He licked my legs, then my neck and face.

I could feel the dog's breath hot on my skin. My life, I knew, now hung on my ability to hold my breath. I was sure that, any second now, I really would die.

"Fritz! Come here!" a man called the dog. A German soldier? A local resident? I had no idea. The dog hung around for a moment more, then ran off to its owner.

I lay prone on the snow, paralyzed, unable to move from the shock, but this was no time to be fickle, I rebuked myself. I need to move on. My cousin reached me from a different direction. Together we walked until, about a half hour later, we saw lights. Slowly we could see homes. We approached the front door. I knocked.

A woman opened, looked us up and down, and signaled for us to come in. She gave us hot tea and a sandwich. The tea warmed our insides; the food calmed our growling stomachs.

The woman sat us down near the fire. Slowly we began to feel our bones thaw. Others in the family suggested we remove our shoes to dry them out, but I politely refused: for over a week I hadn't taken them off and my feet were now very swollen. I could feel how my feet and socks had melded, and was deeply worried that taking my shoes off might mean that I wouldn't be able to put them back on. I moved my feet and legs closer to the fire, and enjoyed the refreshments. This warm reception left me surprised. The woman asked us about our origins. "Refugees from Hungary," I said.

The door opened. SS officers stood in the doorway. There we were, sitting in the living room, while one of the household had quietly gone off to bring the SS. I could hear the officer telling the woman that "a group of Jewish women refugees passed through the village earlier this evening, and almost certainly under the cover of darkness they managed to flee."

My first thought was how lucky I hadn't removed my shoes. Then I'd need to march barefoot!

Rushing us with "Schnell! Schnell!" the soldiers put us into their vehicle and set out. They did not question us, talk to us, or inquire about anything. I was freezing cold and shaking with fear. For sure this would be the end of us now! They'll shoot us without a second thought. I knew that anyone trying to escape had only one fate. as far as the Germans were concerned: death.

We drove for about thirty minutes to a village, then entered a farmyard. What a surprise! We held a constant hope that a miracle could happen and everything could work out alright. That night, after our failed escape, I knew that only a miracle would save us. But it turned out that my group on the death march had been halted at this farm for an overnight stay.

The soldiers went looking for the guards, who were already sound asleep. Seeing us, they shouted, threatened, and warned they'd kill us for trying to escape. We realized that no one had actually realized we'd disappeared into the night. The guards led us to the farm's stables. When they threw the doors open I couldn't believe my eyes: the Germans had confiscated the village's barns, stables and sheds to house the tired prisoners.

We were shoved inside and, when I say shoved, I mean that literally: there was not an inch to spare! The SS and guards had to pitch their strength against the doors in order to close them behind us. The young women stood flush to each other so tightly that they could barely breathe, let alone move. There was no thinking about sitting down. That would have been impossible! And that's how the prisoners were destined to spend the night.

On the other side of the railing stood the horses. I was so tired and wired from the failed escape that all I wanted was to sleep, or sit and lean my head against something.

Looking at the six or seven horses standing there, fresh straw spread beneath them and plenty of room around each of them, I started moving towards them. A very complicated mission but, bit by bit, I made my way forward, step by step, eventually reaching the divider and slipping through to the other side. Calming the horses by gently stroking their backs when they showed signs of agitation, I slowly made myself comfortable, lying down to sleep among them.

In the stable, the young women stared at me gape-mouthed in awe. They begged me to come back to them. "The horses will trample you!" they said. "The horses will kill you!" But I stayed where I was, lying on fresh, clean straw, feeling the warmth of the horse nearby, too tired to be afraid.

Trying to take up as little space as possible, I fell asleep lying on my side and stretched out in a straight line. In the morning I woke with renewed energy. Throughout the night, the horses had quietly stood in their stalls, the women making sure they didn't move and harm me. I slept well.

When the stable doors were opened in the morning, I was blinded by the light reflected from an entire night of pure white snowfall. Shouting "Raus, raus!" and ordering everyone out, guards began clubbing the women on their heads. Those clubs came down incessantly, and the crush in the doorway was horrible. The women wanted to get out, but the crowding caused so many to tumble over them.

One fainted and crumpled into the snow. "Raus, raus!" guards hurried us on. I was drawn into the melee as well, thinking about how the Children of Israel surged out of Egypt, manna falling from heaven to feed them, and here we have snow to eat. We lined up in rows and once again set off in fives through the forest and down the road, guards and dogs our escorts. Efficiently and effectively, our guards fulfilled their jobs to the letter, actually going well above and beyond their instructions.

Wherever they fell, the dead were left, snowflakes slowly covering them. On we marched, huddled into our clothes, our legs swollen, our lips cracked to bleeding, our eyes glazing over. Woe to you if you fell behind! And I do fall. But I get up. Fall again, and stand again, trying to stay with my group. Resting is prohibited. Leaving your row is prohibited. Falling behind is fine if you wish to be shot dead.

The previous night's failed attempt didn't break me. On the contrary, I started planning my next try.

In their efforts to distance us from the frontlines, the Germans led us through all kinds of back paths, without food or water. They would have much preferred had we disappeared into thin air, leaving no trace. At night we continued sleeping in sheds, stables or even under the open sky.

When we passed through German villages, women and men stood outside, wide-eyed with disbelief. The long line of prisoners wound its way down the road, lacking any order. I was thirsty and knew that soon we'd be out of the village and back in the forest. I had to get hold of some water.

Without thinking too much I dashed over to a German woman and begged her for water. She went inside. Moments later she was back with a glass of milk! Unbelievable. I drank. I literally poured it down my throat because there wasn't a moment to spare and what a pity to waste even a drop. "What crime have you committed, that you're all being led like this so cruelly?" she asked me. "Our only crime," I answered, "was that we were born Jewish."

A few moments later, there was the SS officer running towards me, furious with the German woman for daring to give me a drink. I returned her cup and thanked her with my eyes, with my facial gestures, and raced back into my row as the whip came down repeatedly on my back. I told the others in my row that I'd just had a glass of milk. They were convinced I was hallucinating. "Poor thing," their eyes said, because who could have believed it?

On one hand, I felt doomed, yet somewhere inside I knew that, despite the beatings and whippings, I'd make it through and even make it home. I kept repeating this sentence as I took one step after another, all of us marching through cold and snow on empty stomachs. I knew I had to keep my spirits up. But how could I when my stomach ached with emptiness and my lips were dry?

Escape! I need to escape. I must not concede to death. I must not abandon my will to live.

I was sixteen at the time and refused to accept that this was my fate. I marched on, devising plans, daydreaming, my shoes sinking deep into the snow. I daydreamed so deeply that I found myself in the last row, the guard whipping at me, waking me to the bitterness of our reality.

We draw closer to a city. 'Guben' the sign says. Once again, people stop what they're doing, line the streets and gawk at us, guards forbidding them from talking to us, asking questions and, anyhow, we're way too tired to respond even if we had been asked. We are on the verge of starvation, physically exhausted, broken spiritually, and here we are in the Guben camp.

We are in a loop. Once again the barbed wire fences. Once again the watch towers. But at least we have a roof over our heads, and perhaps our declining bodies will be allowed a respite.

GUBEN CAMP

We sat in total silence, each of us focused on our hot meal: a bowl of soup. Then we were herded into a shed and once again we saw bunk beds and blankets. I went up onto one of the higher bunks.

My ankle boots were still on my feet, the very same ones that I'd taken from home. Now I needed to remove them but was so afraid, because the shoe leather, sock and my skin felt like they'd been fused into one; I was scared that taking my socks off would pull my skin off too. But I had no choice. I had to deal with this problem, because who knew what the next day would bring?

Peeling my socks off caused me intense pain, no matter how slowly I progressed. My feet were bloated and lacerated. I fell back onto the bed, drained of energy. The guards closed the doors. At last I could sleep.

Out in the yard the next morning, we learned that the women in this camp worked in a weapons factory in the city of Guben, walking five kilometers each way. We waited near the gate for them to return, eager to see them, hear what they had to tell us, find out how long they were here and what the conditions were like.

Once again, we were searching for family members, relatives, friends, someone we knew, someone with whom we could connect from our previous lives. What did I discover? That my sister Sheindy, who I left behind in Auschwitz never knowing if I'd see her again, was here! Somehow she'd slipped away from Mengele, The Angel of Death.

I couldn't believe it.

After so many months apart, a chance twist of fate brought us together.

After the march of death, the terrible suffering, the agony I'd been through, my fate was at last improving. Soon we'd see each other, be together! My joy was boundless. Knowing that my sister was here brought thoughts of escape even more forcefully to my mind. I had to; I must escape, with Sheindy!

We were closed up in the barracks, having had several hours to roam the yard. I was too excited to lie down in bed. I sat on the floor near the door, waiting for it to be reopened. I kept thinking about my sister, meeting her, the ways in which destiny works: if I hadn't been returned to Auschwitz after Kraków, I wouldn't have found her the first time, and if I hadn't been on the death march and come here, I wouldn't have met her this second time.

***

Writing brings memories to the surface which seem to have been long since erased, but writing also puts me in a state of tense concentration, and often I write without pause as a way of calming my emotions.

***

When the doors opened I raced over to my sister's room, others having already told me where she could be found. Her spot was on the third bunk up. Like a whirlwind I tore into her room and screamed. "Sheindy!" She stared at me in complete shock. Coming down from the bed too fast in her disbelief and excitement, she fell and hurt her leg. But we threw our arms around each other and hugged and kissed and wept, astonished and thankful that we were together again.

My sister wore the gray prisoners' dress and a coat with a red stripe, the familiar mark of a concentration camp inmate. She also wore clogs without socks. Having left Greenberg extremely well-padded in spare clothes, I was able to share my treasures: a sweater, shirts, pajama pants, socks, and several other items. She was thrilled. Now my sister's body would be warm, and that warmed the cockles of my heart.

For hours we told each other of the experiences we'd been through since meeting in Auschwitz, but lights out loomed and here in this place following orders was imperative to stay alive. We not only wanted to survive; we didn't want to do anything that might separate us again. I went back to my block and slept really well for the first time in a long, long while.

The open wound on my sister's foot had me deeply concerned. The next day after work we went to the camp infirmary where it was bandaged, no questions asked.

One thing was absolutely clear to me: we were not going to be split up again. I would do everything possible, and even the impossible, to get both of us out of this camp. We would escape together. No proper plan came to mind yet but, in our current circumstances, it was also clear to me that we'd need to make a snap decision, taking advantage of circumstances as they presented themselves. I didn't share my thoughts with anyone, afraid of informers. I didn't even tell my sister much, just spoke in general terms, and asked her to cooperate with me and trust me if that moment arrived.

Some days after our arrival in Guben we were informed that my group would be leaving the camp and my sister's would stay to work in the factory. I needed to decide quickly on an escape plan that would get us both out of the camp. It was truly an impossible task but I decided to trust my instincts.

There was no other option.

"Look after your sister." Tateh's last words constantly echoed in my thoughts. I also remembered how, when standing on the train station platform at Auschwitz, Sheindy naturally ran to our Mameh, and Mameh instructing her firmly. "Go back to your sister Hilda. She'll look after you." So far I hadn't been able to fulfill my parents' request because forces greater than I could overcome had forced us apart. But this time I knew I'd move fast. I was determined to get Sheindy into my group, no matter what!

I was sitting with Sheindy in her block when the announcement came over the loudspeakers. "Everyone out for roll call." It was also announced that my group would be leaving in an hour. In the center of my sister's room stood a square table of about 120 x 120 centimeters. I waited until everyone had gone out, holding onto my sister's hand to keep her back, then I pushed Sheindy under the table and covered it with her blanket. I asked her not to move until I returned.

Quickly I joined my group, standing in a row. SS guards counted us as well as the girls from Sheindy's group, then counted again, and a third time, finding it impossible to believe that one prisoner was missing. Once it became clear to them that someone was not at roll call, they decided to search the entire camp, especially the rooms. My heart pounded. My legs turned to jelly. They went into my sister's room and searched: under mattresses and under beds, and checked again, and eventually the SS officer walked over to the table where my sister was hiding, pounded on it with his fist, and shouted. "Where can that Jewish prisoner be? We must find her!"

Meanwhile we had been released from roll call so that searches could be conducted. I stood near my sister's barracks, watching from the sidelines, wondering how on earth she was holding up under the table: of course she could glimpse and hear those boots approaching and distancing, and hear their barked orders. They ran about as though they had gone mad: "She must be found dead or alive!" one SS officer screamed repeatedly. "She can't just fly off!"

Surrounded by an electrified fence, outfitted with watch towers and machine guns directed towards the yard, and guards who patrolled all day and night, there was no escaping. Yet they searched along the fence line, employed their hounds and, of course, found nothing because Sheindy was still under the table hidden by the blanket. I was so scared for her but I was determined to implement my plan, no matter how crazy it seemed.

SS officers continued hunting until, at some point, they gave up and called off the search effort. They had no choice but to stop because our group had to get moving; the announcement had said that we're leaving Guben immediately. I took a well-studied shortcut, literally throwing myself into Sheindy's barracks, diving in through the window before the other girls reentered. I hurrying my sister out from under the table so that no one would see where she'd been and report it. My sister was in a state of shock, not understanding what had just happened.

There was no time for explanations. I tugged at her forcefully to get her out from under the table and, through the window into the yard, told her to stay right next to me the whole time. I pulled her into the roll call and my group. Trembling and pale, she stood in my row of five, which of course caused a new problem: now the row numbered six! None of the women there know that Sheindy was my sister.

SS officers dashed about in a state of high tension and nervous energy, shouting orders, dogs barking, guards at the ready, and there we were, still six in the row instead of five.

At last the gates were pushed open.

We started walking, moving forward slowly. I glanced at Sheindy. Her eyes were fearful; her face was ashen. But talking was forbidden. I didn't want to hold her hand: that would indicate I knew her. We kept our gaze glued to the gate, as though the fuss in the camp was of no interest to us, and kept walking. Right before we reached the gate, one of the women left my row and walked back to one of the last rows.

I breathed a sigh of relief, but knew there could be countless more obstacles to overcome until we'd passed through the gate. What if one of the Germans realized the young woman in my row was not from my group and pulled Sheindy out? I blocked the thought from my mind to avoid considering the consequences. So on we went, one step, another, towards the gates.

None of us had any idea where we were headed but what mattered most to me was that I'd managed to get Sheindy out of the camp. We were called to a halt in front of the gate as usual, and our rows of five were counted: five, ten, fifteen, twenty...

The SS officer counting our row didn't look at our faces. We were of no interest to him as people. His focus was on ensuring that the number of women exiting matched the number on his lists. So he counted each row as the women went through the gate. Another few steps, another two steps, one more... and we were through to the other side!

Amazing. We'd done it. My sister was with me. We still couldn't speak to each other, but I allowed myself to quickly touch her fingertips as a sign of reassurance: you can relax now, the danger of getting you out is over and we're still together. Hallelujah!

It was still too soon to look at her, especially since I feared we would both be too emotional: she might smile at me, or cry to release the tension, and that would arouse suspicion. "Tateh!" I wanted to scream, "Look! Sheindy's with me at last!"

Night began to fall and on we marched, still with no idea of our destination. Was this another death march or were we being taken somewhere? Eventually we reached a station where open cattle cars awaited us. Midwinter, snow falling without a break, freezing cold, and the Germans had prepared open cattle cars for us.

We sat huddled against each other inside, wrapped in our blankets to provide as much protection as possible from the bone-chilling cold. Some more orders from the SS and the train pulled away. Sheindy and I were wrapped together in one blanket. We were so tired that we fell asleep.

In the morning I couldn't move the blanket off us. It had frozen solid. We barely managed to wiggle our way out from under a night of constant snowing. We encountered a horrible sight in the morning. Two young women had frozen to death, their heads swollen like balloons. Sheindy was in bad shape, cold, apathetic, the sore on her foot aching. She just wanted to be left alone; she wanted to sleep.

Only days earlier we'd at last found each other. Was I going to lose her now? What could I do to help her? I had no idea. I had whisked her away from the camp into this life-endangering situation. If the Germans had caught us then, we'd both have been murdered on the spot, but here we were. No, I wasn't giving up on her now.

LEAVING GUBEN

While in Guben I'd heard rumors from other girls who worked in the city: the Russians were coming closer, the Germans were fleeing. The noise from the tanks was clearly heard but now we were once again being distanced from the liberation we yearned. I also heard about the situation inside Germany from the guards with us in the carriages. They spoke with each other constantly, freely and loudly, not seeming to care if we heard. They complained of the cold in these open cattle cars. I listened closely to an argument amongst several of them. Every sentence held details precious to someone planning an escape. I had a feeling that these snippets would one day prove useful to Sheindy and me. I decided to make another escape attempt, this time with my sister and cousin.

As with our previous attempt, my logic said there was nothing to lose. If we were caught, our chances of survival were the same as our chances out here: a bullet to the head, or death by freezing and starvation, as we were given any food. Of one thing I was certain: at the very least I had to try, for the sake of our family and our parents.

Meanwhile the guards had been told that two women had frozen to death. Two soldiers entered the carriage: one grabbed one of the dead women by her armpits and the other grabbed her legs; they did a quick one, two, three count and heaved her out. I was horrified. Is that what awaited us on this journey? Sheindy had already surrendered to her condition and fate.

Would we see one or more of us being tossed out like a sack of potatoes every day? Every bone in my body fumed. Is this what my sister deserved? What I deserved? What the others with us deserved?

There was no other option but to devise an escape plan.

On and on the train rolled, racing along the tracks, semi-conscious young women sitting, huddled under frozen blankets, traveling to nowhere. I suppose the only person with any inkling of our destination was the engine driver. Not even the guards seemed to know where we were headed. Food was handed out. Sheindy recovered a little. Of course, I'd kept my ideas to myself, but now I knew I'd have to share the secret with Sheindy.

She didn't express any opposition. Actually, in retrospect, I'm not even sure she even fully comprehended what I was saying, but I asked her for one moment of grace – when I give the signal to jump from the train, you must not resist nor ask questions. We pulled the frozen blanket over our heads and whispered, making sure no one could hear us.

My cousin was also brought into the loop. I told her that Sheindy and I had made the decision to flee and, although it seemed like a crazy idea, I had to at least try to get us off this death train.

Dehydration had caused deep cracks on my lips. Moistening them by catching a bit of snow, I signaled to Sheindy and my cousin to do the same. Our world was reduced to nothing but snow.

Now I waited tensely for the right opportunity. The next night, the train's wheels slowed and eventually it jolted to a halt. 'Celle' read the station's sign. We were in the region of Hanover, in northwest Germany.

THE GREAT ESCAPE

The guards left the carriage unattended, going into the station to get themselves some food before the journey continued. "Now!" I said to Sheindy and my cousin. "We need to do it now!"

I didn't give them much time to think. Picking up my sister's clogs, I tossed them out, then gave her a leg-up to the carriage's side and told her to jump. A matter of life or death. She did. I jumped after her. My cousin also landed safely. Marika, Sheindy's friend, who had no inkling of my plan, saw us and without giving the matter a second thought, jumped too.

When other young women saw us jumping, their courage was suddenly roused and they also began hurling themselves over the sides, scattering every which way, each running in a different direction.

Upon returning to the carriages, the guards saw they were half empty. Aiming at random, they started shooting into the night but couldn't see us. Suddenly a voice rang through the night: a shout of pain. A woman had been hit. Another scream of pain from the same general direction. Instantly we stopped and changed our direction, distancing ourselves from the rest of the escapees.

We ran wherever our legs took us. Snow continued coming down. We were fearful of being hunted down by dogs, or that our footprints would show in the fresh powder. But we couldn't hear dogs, nor shots. We presumed that the Germans had found some of the others and rounded them up but had lost us. On we plodded but, after about an hour, realized we were back at the station. We were so sorry that we'd lost that precious time only to find ourselves at our starting point. We turned towards a different direction and began to run.

Easier said than done. Clogs are far from conducive to running. Snow clings to them and, if we wanted to keep progressing, once in while it was necessary to stop and bang them against each other to remove the snow. Marika hadn't known about our plan to escape but, once she realized what we were up to, she chose to stay with us.

There was another big problem with Marika. She only spoke Hungarian, having come from an area of Hungary that spoke no other languages. This was a big drawback, since we all spoke fairly reasonable German, certainly sufficient to be easily understood.

How interesting that people who had lost all hope, lost their will to live, lost interest in their surroundings, can suddenly revive! Despite my sister wearing wooden shoes and having an extremely painful sore on her foot, she managed to run, to not ask questions, to not look back and, most of all, didn't even utter a word in complaint.

We meandered into the dark, cold, snowy night. If not for a spot of moonlight reflecting on the snow, we wouldn't have seen a thing in the pitch black.

The fear hadn't left us but I was hoping that, because they were in such a hurry the Germans, already running late, had given up their search for us and had moved on. I guessed they may have collected some of the wounded closest to the train, but left the rest of us behind.

We passed the city without seeing a soul. We walked near the houses, moving quickly and, in no time, we were beyond the cluster of homes. Our goal was to reach a village so remote and secluded that they hadn't yet heard about the Jewish prisoners, the concentration camps, or the Auschwitz furnaces.

Our immense will to survive was so extraordinarily powerful. With a tad of luck, I thought, and a bit of a story that sounded reasonable, maybe we could find a way to last through the rest of the war. Perhaps my plan appeared somewhat childish, but in times of dire distress and despair, people will do the most bizarre things.

Meanwhile, we'd clearly made headway and were very far from the train station.

We walked through fields with no idea where we were but, glancing back, our footprints were easily visible in the snow.

Sheindy was barely able to walk because of her foot, the cold, and her hunger, but she said nothing. Dropping down to let her climb onto my shoulders, we continued like that until we reached a stream where we stopped, rested and considered our options. If we followed the banks and the Nazis were still hunting for us, they'd find us because of the marks we left in the snow; but if we crossed the stream, not even the smartest dog would find us.

It was almost dawn. We looked for a path, a road, knowing we had to get out of these snowfields that led nowhere. We decided to try crossing the stream, its frozen surface glittering like a mirror. We had no idea how thick the ice was, or how deep the water might be, but there was no time to think let alone philosophize. A decision had to made, and fast.

As we descend the bank, we notice how soft and deep the snow is, and walk slowly and carefully to be sure we won't lose our shoes in the snow's grip. We're so tense that we no longer feel hungry or thirsty. We want only one thing: to reach the stream safely. We know that what we're doing is crazy, not normal, but has there been anything logical and reasonable about our actions thus far?

There's no going back and we need to hurry, to keep moving forward.

Cautiously we plod on. The water reached our waists. At this rate, the water will soon be up to our shoulders but we're almost midway across the stream. We need to keep going. Regret is pointless at this point: from where we've just come, there's nothing but certain death. We've slogged through mud, our faces and arms lacerated by branches, and my sister is still in her clogs. That was my biggest worry: I have to make sure she doesn't lose her shoes. With great trepidation we wade on.

We're in up to our necks. I need to poke my sister's chin upwards to be sure she doesn't drink the stream water. But we've passed the halfway point and the water level continuously drops. The layer of mud on the stream bed is thick and sticky, sucking us down. Again I pray that my sister doesn't lose her shoes. Another few steps. We've done it! We're safely on the other side of the stream!

The will to survive is one of the most powerful of human instincts.

We find ourselves in Germany, an unfamiliar country, without parents, without family, without anyone whose advice we could seek; the only thing that matters is staying alive. We stand there, wet, dripping, frozen, exhausted as dawn begins to light the sky.

Which way do we go now? We're hungry, thirsty, our lips are dry and swollen from the cold.

"Let's eat snow," I say. "We're only at the start of this journey, and we need to keep our strength up. Snow is water, and water is life, so maybe it will help us." Every part of our bodies quivers from the cold. We can't feel our hands or feet. But we have to make a decision: which way should we go?

Looking around, I see large flakes of snow falling to the ground. Nothing but one great expanse of snow. My legs are swollen and aching from the cold, and my sister can barely walk in her clogs.

I gaze upwards. 'I will lift up mine eyes unto the hills, From whence cometh my help?' I remember the psalm's words. I point. "We're going that way," I say without having any idea what lies ahead.

By now Sheindy had lost all feeling in her legs but, like an obedient soldier, she marched on. Suddenly I noticed a long road not far from us, dotted by people moving in a manner that seemed to indicate they were riding bicycles. Judging by the early hour of the morning, perhaps they were going from a village to work in the city. In that case, there must be a village not far away. This startling conclusion encouraged us to begin walking in the direction from which the bicycle riders were coming.

Slowly we approached them, but walked on, looking neither right nor left, but raising our heads and looking straight ahead as though we, too, were hurrying off to some place. They were gawking at us with amazement. "Who are you, and where have you come from, and where are you going?" their eyes seemed to ask.

We must have looked ghostly in our wet clothing, which clung frozen on our starving, frail, exhausted bodies. Our legs kept moving, step after step, but we couldn't feel them. I knew that if we didn't find somewhere to bed down for the night, our situation would be dire. We had to find a place to stay until the enemy army would liberate us. Would we get to see that great day? We moved away from the bike riders who we concluded, from snippets we could hear, must be German laborers, and continued towards the village.

On the way we passed a forest. I told my little gang to go in despite a sign saying, 'Entry Forbidden.' We needed to rest a little. I hoped that the forest would be clear of soldiers: if it wasn't, we'd be fair game. Carefully we entered, looking about, but didn't see a soul. We went in further, deep among the trees to be sure we couldn't be spotted from the road. What luck that it was a sunny midwinter day!

We found a broad tree, cleared the snow away, tied our soaking blanket to its branches above our heads, and sat down, leaning against the trunk. It wasn't long before we'd fallen into an exhausted sleep.

We slept for several hours before waking to a din. An elderly German man was cutting wood not far from us. We sat in complete silence, on the lookout to be sure no one could see us as we tried to dry our clothes. No one said a word about food because whatever we'd had in our pockets had also become sodden when we crossed the stream. Once again we were left with no choice but to eat snow... as much as we wanted.

Unexpectedly, the courage I'd roused when I jumped out of the train suddenly left me. I began doubting this escape: had I done the right thing by bringing my sister, who was unwell, with me?

In silence we waited until the woodchopper left, then folded the blanket, smoothed our clothes down, and set out to leave the forest. We weren't far from the village now. I looked at our odd gaggle: my cousin, my sister, and her friend: weak, fatigued young women, starving, in need of support and assistance.

At a certain point I stopped the group and turned to Marika. "Here we need to part ways," I said. We decided that she'd say she's a Hungarian exile and we, my sister, our cousin and I, would be German and that I'd be our speaker.

Once again we found ourselves at a crossroads. "Which way should we go now?" Sheindy asked. "Right," I whispered without the faintest clue where it might lead us.

GARSSEN

We walked through the village streets in the dark, shivering from the cold. We looked at each of the houses, trying to figure out which door to approach. One looked too nice. "We won't be wanted there," I said to the others. Another looked too much like a hovel. We walked down the street, house by house, searching for the right one.

Eventually we came across one that was neither too large nor too flashy. Knocking at the door, our hearts leapt with hope that we'd be given food and drink. Beyond that, we had no expectations at all.

An older woman opened the door. She studied us slowly, from head to foot. My heart raced, my knees turned to mush and I kept wondering if, any second now, she'd send us away. But no, she gestured to us to enter and, once inside, asked if we were displaced. "Yes," we said, knowing for certain that she absolutely did not mean Jewish displaced persons! She sat us at the table without asking anything further, went to the kitchen and, some minutes later, returned with a tray bearing three glasses of hot tea and two slices of bread spread with confiture for each of us!

This was a true royal feast as far as we were concerned. I held my glass tightly in both hands, feeling the hot liquid spread through my arms to the rest of my body, and the slices of fresh bread with strawberry preserve tasted like paradise.

She said not a word as we ate. Patiently, she sat with us and gave us time to enjoy the food. Then she said she couldn't be of further help but promised she'd take us to someone who could.

"Who is this man who can help us?" I dared ask.

"The Burgermeister, head of the village." The woman explained that he was caring for refugees entering the village and would 'help you all out.' Was she speaking the truth? Was she about to turn us in?

Fear crept into my heart. It seemed too good to be true, and too simple to be real. I was on the verge of desperation but knew I had to keep playing this game. We absolutely had to find a place to stay until liberation. After all, our efforts to escape and our treacherous adventure through the snow, the stream, and suffering the elements were to that end.

Our hostess took us to the Burgermeister, who lived in the house we thought was too lavish and had decided to bypass. The woman presented us to him, saying we were refugees who'd arrived a short while ago, most likely on foot because we looked so very tired and hungry. She asked him to help find us somewhere to stay. Then she turned back to walk home. We thanked her before she left us, bidding a warm goodbye.

Serving as the village mayor, the Burgermeister was tall, had a large round face, was constantly smiling, and seemed to be kindhearted. Or at least that was the impression he made. He invited us to sit, leaned back in his chair, studied us, and began bombarding us with questions. *That's it*, I thought, not for the first time, *we're finished*. He asked where we were from, how we arrived, by train or vehicle, or perhaps by horse-drawn wagon? Where were our parents? Why were we alone? To him we were a very odd phenomenon: youngsters with no parents who had shown up in his village. He was a friendly, talkative chap and truly curious about what had happened to us.

Now the big moment had come, the one I feared most, the moment I had to tell our story, knowing it had to be convincing. If it wasn't, we were done for. There I sat, sixteen years old, facing an adult not only with life experience but respected as the Burgermeister, the lives of three young Jews balancing on my shoulders.

As though something was blocking my voice, I had trouble getting started. But at last I pulled myself together and invented a cover story, leaving my family and all who were dear to me out of it. Blatantly and bluntly, I lied. We are from the city of Guben, our mother died when we were still little and our father, enlisted as a soldier in the German army some years ago, hasn't been heard from for many months now. Since most of the people had left that city due to the fear that the Russians would conquer the entire region, and because all our neighbors also fled, we decided to leave too, not wanting to be there on our own.

Upon reaching the Guben station, I continued, the station workers told us to place our belongings in the last carriage which would vacate seats in the passenger carriages. In fact, this was one of the snippets I'd heard the guards discussing on our journey from Guben to Celle; it came in useful now but the Burgermeister didn't need to know that, of course.

Once the train started moving, the station workers disconnected the last carriage from the rest of the train. All our bags and suitcases were there, but we didn't know about that until we'd arrived. The Burgermeister's eyes showed interest and, of course, this was yet another excerpt I'd overhead from the guards' conversation. And that's how we were left with absolutely nothing: no clothes, no documents, and no money.

On I talked, each moment waiting for earth to open up and swallow us whole from the lies I was spewing. If this tale helped us survive, I thought, then let it be. So I was quite surprised to hear the Burgermeister say that he'd heard many similar stories from refugees who'd made their way to the village who'd also complained of how the station workers had basically robbed them of their possessions using this method.

And that was how I discovered that the village had absorbed

numerous refugees who'd fled in fear of the Russians, leaving their homes and belongings behind, fleeing with almost nothing at all, and then having even that stolen.

Once I stopped talking, he didn't ask anything more. Instead, he said how sorry he was that our father hadn't given any signs of life for so long. He promised to write to the German Ministry of Defense seeking information about our father. He was sure, he said, that he'd be able to find him.

The conversation coming to an end, he said he'd take us to the 'Judenheim' where we'd be able to sleep the night. I had no idea what that was: the words translated literally meant 'Jews' house.' Was it possible that prior to the war there'd been a Jewish community center or school here, and the building's name had stuck? The implications horrified me, but I said nothing.

We entered the building and found it filled with German refugees. Every room was packed with beds. Exchanging a few words with the house mother, the Burgermeister asked her to look after us, explaining that we were orphans: our mother had died and our father was a German soldier. Instantly, I could see how our value rose in her eyes.

The house mother handed us blankets, clean sheets, and allocated us beds. We were given a hot meal. When the food tray was handed to each of us, we couldn't believe our eyes: it held an array of delicacies. The Burgermeister never left our side for a moment, taking personal care of us to be sure we had what we needed. Being so unused to such kindness, I viewed it as suspect and became fearful: was he onto us?

We could only wait and see. But I had such a hard time believing our good fortune and how, within a matter of hours, our situation had so dramatically improved. I'm sure our rather Aryan appearance also contributed to making our story more believable.

Before the Burgermeister left, he asked us if 'you little girls,' as he referred to us, were satisfied. I thanked him warmly, praising everything he'd done for us, but I did have one request, if possible: my sister's leg was hurt and needed treatment. Immediately the Burgermeister sent one of the Hitler-Jugend to call the doctor. We would soon discover that working in this building were adolescents of the Hitler Youth Movement whose job it was to help assimilate refugees.

These youngsters, male and female alike, wore the Hitler-Jugend symbol on their sleeves. Seeing them churned my stomach, but we needed to play the game, thanking the Burgermeister again for the excellent treatment Sheindy received. For three days she lay in a clinic bed, visited daily by the doctor, attended to by the Hitler-Jugend, their armbands displaying the swastika, bringing her meals and drinks to her bed to ensure the leg could rest and heal. What irony.

What would become of us? Where would this kindness lead? I had no idea, but at least for now our situation was far better than we could ever have imagined.

In a single hour I'd changed identity, dismissing my Jewishness, my family, my people. From now on I was a German refugee in the village of Garssen and I had to be sure not to make even the slightest mistake, nor ever allow myself to become distracted. Alert, that's what I had to be, constantly vigilant to everything happening, around the clock, day and night. I am German and I must not forget that for a moment. We are little girls without parents, which drew attention to us. Everyone wanted to help and they were piling on their love and concern.

German refugees did not work, of course. Volunteers prepared the German refugees' meals and the youngsters of the Hitler-Jugend tidied and cleaned the house. Volunteers really enjoyed pampering us.

One day Sheindy's friend showed up at the Judenheim. Marika! Of course we could not talk to each other, but I raised my eyebrows as though to ask: what's going on? She answered with a tiny hand gesture: she doesn't know. The building was full of people and finding an isolated spot where we could talk privately was impossible. Some days later we no longer saw her there.

Once Sheindy's wound had healed, we visited the Burgermeister to present a request. It was difficult for us, we said, to sit all day doing nothing. It let us think too much about our father fighting the war and made us very worried. We asked if he could perhaps arrange work for us. It didn't really matter what: we could work in housekeeping or farming. From other German women among the refugees we understood that there was a serious lack of farmhands. We tried to use that rumor to our advantage.

Listening to us patiently, if a little amused, the Burgermeister explained that there was no need for us to work because we were being taken care of, but I wasn't giving in. I asked again and again: could he find us jobs in the farms? It would help us pass the time more easily. He promised to look into finding good families for us, but it may take a little while.

I trusted the Burgermeister. Our interactions with him were good thus far, but I'd begun to feel that being in the Judenheim was becoming increasingly risky. It would be far better if we could distance ourselves from so many people, which would make us less conspicuous and less exposed to questions or the arrival of newcomers who might recognize and endanger us, as Marika's appearance had highlighted. A farm seemed like the best solution.

Some days later, the Burgermeister informed us that two families were happy to take us into their homes. The following day a woman came to take Sheindy and our cousin to one of the homes, and the Burgermeister took me to the second location.

The home belonged to a woman who lived alone; her husband was a soldier on the front lines. I noticed how the German women always emphasized that their soldier husbands were 'on the front.' This woman, whose name I've forgotten, had a number of farm animals in her yard and a small vegetable garden for personal use. She received me warmly; I felt comfortable in her home. She didn't interrogate me. She hardly asked any questions at all. I guess the Burgermeister had already filled her in.

I was shown to my room. What a dream! I helped her with the animals, the field, the chicken coop and the in the house, and even helped her cook. We got along well; no problems surfaced. In the evenings she embroidered tablecloths, and taught me the art of intricate artistic embroidery. How idyllic! Everything would have been fine if not for the neighbors.

Village homes were built very close to one another and neighbors popped in and out frequently. To me it seemed my hostess' neighbors were showing a bit too much interest in me. I needed to deflect questions: about our absent parents, about why we'd chosen this village.

Pressure was mounting by the day. Once again I could feel danger hovering above my head but, for now, I had no other solution.

One day the Burgermeister came to the house, telling me we needed to travel to several city offices to arrange for papers: an identity card, food vouchers, and a German refugee certificate. He added that we'd also be able to receive clothes and shoes.

Shoes! Now that was something. My sister was still dragging her clogs around and often enough they would rouse people's curiosity. It would be worth going, I thought, and not just for the shoes. Who knew when another opportunity might present itself?

One of the Hitler-Jugend kids would accompany us to town, said the Burgermeister, and take us to the various offices, which would make the whole process move ahead faster and more smoothly.

I was scared. All I needed was a Hitler-Jugend kid tagging along with us. On the other hand, how would I manage without him? I thanked the Burgermeister and told him I think we'd be able to manage on our own, and it would actually be fun, a bit of excitement for us, a small adventure. The Burgermeister's suggestion of providing us with a Hitler-Jugend teen as escort was well intentioned but also unsafe for us.

"Don't worry," I reassured him, "we'll find the offices. And I'm sure we'll be back with the necessary documents." But, in my heart, I was wondering: would everything indeed work out alright?

The offices were located in Celle, the place we'd escaped. Here we were returning to the scene of the crime! That thought alone shook me, but the show had to go on.

Some seven kilometers separated Garssen from Celle. How would we get there? That was a serious problem because we had no money. Clearly the Burgermeister hadn't thought this through, nor did we wish to ask him. We didn't want to go by bus either: that was too risky. Our hair, shaved in Auschwitz, was growing back but was still very short, which drew attention. I was afraid that an SS officer might be on the bus and discover us, or perhaps some random man or woman who knew what concentration camp prisoners looked like might start asking questions and cause enough chaos and speculation that we wouldn't be able to return to Garssen.

We decided to deal with the situation on our own. Only if we had no other choice, we'd ask for help. We'd walk there. I asked for all the details, wrote addresses down, and prayed in my heart that we'd succeed in this challenging mission.

We left the village at first light. Laborers rode their bikes to town. We walked, but this time in the same direction as they were going. None of them asked us anything. They just stared at us.

It was a long way, and seemingly longer when walking, but eventually we reached the city's outskirts. We noticed people standing around chatting, laughing, hurrying to their jobs. A bustling city. We walked to its business center, checking around us all the time. Two SS officers were coming towards us. That hat, those gleaming boots. We shuddered.

There was nowhere to flee, nor any way of doing it subtly. We had to keep walking, our hearts pounding. I told Sheindy to raise her head and walk as though she belonged. The two SS officers were coming closer. Were they staring at us or was I imagining it? And then they passed us. "Keep walking," I whispered, "do not turn to look back." And we were safe.

Later we saw countless SS officers, eventually taking the sight of them in stride. We hurried, not so quickly that we'd raise anyone's suspicion, but not so slowly that we wouldn't complete what we'd set out to do, which would mean that we'd have to return and go through this ordeal a second time. We showed the address to a woman who pointed us in the general direction. At some point we needed to ask for finer details. I nodded in thanks so that we said as little as possible and not to spend too much time with the person giving instructions: we didn't want to encourage any conversations. In that way we managed to reach each of the offices.

One office issued us food cards. The Ministry of the Interior provided identity cards. A third office produced documents certifying that we were German refugees. No special problems were encountered yet. At last there was just one office left – where we would receive shoes and clothes. With no great difficulty we found the storeroom in a kind of aid center for needy refugees.

Two clerks worked there. One kept staring at us. She hardly looked away. Perhaps she sensed something was odd but couldn't put her finger on it. Her constant gaze made us feel extremely uncomfortable. I handed over our new identity cards and the note we'd received in the village allotting us shoes and clothes but the clerk seemed jumpy. She began asking questions in a very aggressive manner, and made it clear she wanted precise answers. So I related our story again, adding a bit here, dropping a bit there, half-truths and half-lies, hoping to get safely through what felt like an interrogation. Meanwhile the other clerk brought out a packet of clothing. Sheindy tried on a pair of shoes.

"What an odd accent these girls have," the doubting clerk noted.

"True," answered the clerk who was so kindly helping, "but don't you know that each part of Germany has a different dialect?"

"That's true," the doubting one immediately shot back, "but theirs is extremely odd."

An argument broke out between the clerk defending us and the one attacking us. There was no way we were going to hang around for that to reach its conclusion. We signed the papers on the desk, took the packages, Sheindy already wearing the new shoes, thanked them, and left as fast as we could without seeming impolite.

Outside we breathed a sigh of relief. We had gotten through all the tasks, including clothes and shoes. Unbelievable. I wanted to run and shout with joy, but no, of course it was far safer to keep a low profile. Thank goodness we succeeded.

The streets were filled with SS officers. I was afraid that after having achieved everything that would keep us safe we could lose it all in an instant, that an SS officer would suddenly notice us, would ask himself whether we didn't look like we'd escaped a concentration camp. The best thing, I whispered to Sheindy and our cousin, would be for us to get out of the city as fast as we could and back to the village. And right then my sister told me she was starving hungry. What should we do now?

We hadn't brought any food with us, nor did we have any money. I remembered hearing other refugees in the village talking about soup kitchens run by German volunteers at various locations in the city where hot food was served... only to German refugees of course. I decided to look for one of those places, but not at any price. If we found one easily, fine. If we didn't, we'd head back to the village.

Wandering through the city center we suddenly noticed a small side street where people had queued up: children, the elderly, women with babies. Yes, we'd found a public soup kitchen. So we joined the line, and each of us received a hot meal. The dining hall was crowded, the noise was extremely loud, but we found a place to sit down.

I constantly scanned the room, fearful of someone following us, or examining us, or that we'd exaggerated with our self-confidence by coming to a public place like this. Suddenly I noticed a thin, frail man sitting on the floor in a corner. He kept eyeing us.

Right away I knew what he was hiding. Although dressed in civilian clothing, they were insufficiently warm to protect him from the winter's cold and snow. His hair was so short that it barely covered his scalp. He made no attempt to approach us. Like us, he was a Jewish escapee. I thought it best we keep our distance.

We finished eating, signaled acknowledgment to the man with the slightest of head movements, and left to begin our long walk to the village.

Once we were back 'home' we visited the Burgermeister in his office. Gathering the papers together, I placed them on his desk. First he glanced at them, then checked them thoroughly, his amazement growing by the minute. "It takes people weeks to get their papers in order because some problem always comes up, and here, look, you've done it all in one day! I'm impressed. I'm very proud of you."

The Burgermeister asked if we were happy with the families we'd been allocated. "We're very pleased," I said warmly, "but we're also a bit disappointed, because we thought we'd be placed on a large farm. We're young," I added when his eyebrows went up a little in surprise, "and I thought we'd be able to support the war effort during this period when there's such a lack of able hands."

He repeated his earlier response: that there really was no

need for us to work, but since he sees that we're somewhat persistent about the idea, he'd look for work for us on a large farm. Obviously, the well-meaning Burgermeister had no idea that we were seeking a way to safeguard ourselves by distancing from the village and so many people trying to help who they thought of as 'those poor refugees.'

He also told us that he'd written a letter to the German Ministry of Defense asking for information about our father and received a response: he was registered as missing. The Burgermeister expressed his sympathy and added that he'd continue looking for him. I was sure he would. We left his office, papers in hand. Out in the street I checked them once more and deep fear engulfed me. I was horrified. Here's what our papers noted:

Father's name: Shemaya Herscowitz

Mother's name: Leah Herscowitz

Sister's name: Margarete Herscowitz

My name: Hilda Herscowitz

Our "sister's" name: Mali Herscowitz

We'd included our cousin as a sister, giving the name "Mali," short for her Jewish name, Malcah, and using our surname.

What kinds of German surnames were these! Terrible. I was convinced that the Burgermeister had found us out now and was laughing behind our backs. How had I not thought of changing the names on our certificates? I should have given far more consideration to the matter and its consequences! Once again I was scared to death.

We'd changed our country, our identity, and our language, pretty much overnight; we'd been allocated adoptive families; and the Burgermeister was very fatherly towards us, making sure we lacked for nothing. Had I just put it all at risk? Had I brought calamity upon us all? What might happen if they discover the truth?

But there was nothing I could do about it now. It wasn't possible to return to the Ministry of the Interior to change our names. For the umpteenth time, I repeated the phrase I'd used so far to keep my spirits up: 'the show must go on.' A tiny spark of hope colored the horizon of my thoughts and fears: perhaps the Burgermeister really did not have any suspicions about us, otherwise why would he be so helpful? Perhaps everything was fine, nonetheless? We had no choice but to wait things out, not lose hope, and not capitulate to worry. I took comfort in the fact that our certificates specifically noted our acceptably Aryan appearances: blond hair, blue eyes.

Day after day went by as we waited for some small miracle that would get us safely out of the village. Life was fine in the home of the woman I was sent to; she had no children and was happy for the company and, over time, we even developed friendly relations. She repeatedly spoke of her husband on the front lines, and that her family lived very far from her. One day she even told me that a bloody battle had occurred on a particular front, forcing the German soldiers to retreat.

I listened closely, rejoicing in my heart, but outwardly empathizing with her so convincingly that she immediately tried to soothe my angst, saying that she was sure things would work out alright and Germany would win.

One morning the Burgermeister invited us to his office to share some good news. With a huge smile he said he'd found a large farm in the village of Ohe, about six kilometers from Garssen. Ohe was tiny, comprised of a mere seven families, but each of them ran a large farm. Perfect, I thought. He'd found two kind families to take us in, and reassured us that we'd be well looked after there, while indeed contributing to the war effort.

Here was the miracle we'd hoped for, the best news we could imagine. Of course we agreed to the suggestion right away, thanking him for his concern.

The woman I'd been living with was very sorry I was leaving her, and tried convincing me to stay. I explained that I certainly would have liked to continue being with her, but the Burgermeister was transferring us elsewhere. Of course I never let on that I was the one who'd asked for our transfer. She'd love it if I was able to come and visit occasionally, she said, and I promised to even though I knew I was never going to come back.

My hostess' neighbors were sorry to hear of my departure. She packed a hefty bundle of clothing for me, saying that I'd surely be needing them in the coming cold winter months. That Sunday morning a wagon hitched to two horses halted outside her house, driven by our new employer-of-sorts, Mr. Laupper. The Burgermeister, who'd also come to be sure matters were properly taken care of, introduced us, noting that our documents were in order, including food cards.

He mentioned again that he'd sent a letter inquiring about our father, but had so far not received any answer. Now he turned to Mr. Laupper and asked him to check every so often on our behalf, additionally asking him to be in touch with him periodically to update him on our welfare because he wanted to be sure that the 'little German girls' were doing well. We thanked the Burgermeister repeatedly for his appreciated assistance when we first arrived, and waved as the wagon pulled out, perhaps just a little sorry that we were leaving him.

By this point I was certain he had no idea of our secret and indeed had helped us out of the goodness of his heart.

ON THE WAY TO OHE

The sound of tanks grew increasingly thunderous. We realized that the front was moving closer and further into Germany proper. During our last few days in Garssen, countless soldiers had begun appearing, officers being billeted with families, and regular soldiers put up in barns and stables. The entire village was turning into a German military camp, with more coming by the day, tired, wounded, on foot and in vehicles. For us, it was best not be in Garssen.

We just have to keep up the good impression, I repeated to myself. A bit longer. Liberation can't be far away. Perhaps we'll survive. Perhaps we'll get to start new chapters in our lives, and things will go back to being good. And so we traveled with the man on the wagon, the horses galloping along, us three youngsters huddled on the back seat.

Mr. Laupper sang songs to lift our spirits, encouraging us to join in. It never occurred to him that we didn't know these German songs. He described Ohe, the seven families living there, the creek passing through the village, and how it's a fun place to swim in summer. He tried to draw us into a conversation but we stayed quiet. The village, based on what he said, seemed like a lovely, picturesque place. I was thinking about the new families we'd be settled with, and the fact that we need to start our whole life story over again. Despite being fully aware of the risks constantly surrounding us, outwardly we acted very calmly and normally.

For about an hour we passed snow-covered forests and fields. "We've arrived in Ohe," Mr. Laupper announced at last. Looking around, I saw several homes with large spaces between them. Excellent: no neighbors so close that they could constantly pepper us with questions that would require us to constantly be on guard. Mr. Laupper flicked the reins. A few minutes later we halted at his farm.

We followed him into a cowshed where a number of large, plump cows lay, then walked on behind him to its far end where Mr. Laupper opened a door... right into the kitchen! The Laupper's home and cowshed were linked by this shared door, making it easier to reach the cows for milking. The kitchen had a second door which opened onto the yard.

Two women were waiting for us in the kitchen: Mrs. Laupper and Mrs. Lochte. They stopped chatting and turned their gaze towards us. Then came the usual questions for which we provided the usual answers. By now we'd become accomplished at responding. The two women didn't pressure us, and were very sympathetic towards the poor refugees who'd lost their family and home. After discussion between them, the women decided that Sheindy and my cousin would stay with the Lauppers and I'd join Mrs. Lochte on her farm.

During this interview I'd remained silent other than answering when addressed but, after the decisions had been reached, I felt I had to ask one thing: how far the two farms were from each other. The women reassured me that it was only five-minute walk between the fields and that Mrs. Lochte's home was the one closest to the Lauppers. Clearly the families were on good terms and would most likely not prevent us from meeting up with each other when possible. And so I wished my sister well, and joined Mrs. Lochte for the walk to her farm.

Along the way, Mrs. Lochte told me about her family: three sons, two of whom were recruited, and the youngest, eleven, was still living at home. I was thinking that, from my perspective, two sons in the army could be risky: what if they were given furlough and came home to visit? Once again I decided that this was a thought that could be laid aside for now, and I'd worried about it if and when the situation arose.

Meanwhile, we'd reached the Lochte farm, where a large yard held several kinds of farm machinery. "Here's the cowshed," Mrs. Lochte pointed, "and there's the stables. Laborers live in this building, and that one at the end is our family's home."

We went inside. Mr. Lochte came towards us in greeting. He was in his sixties and received me warmly, saying he hoped I'd be happy with them. I hoped so too. As he spoke, Mrs. Lochte set the table and invited me to join them for dinner. Their young son shyly came over, reserved, examining me, but saying nothing and keeping a wary distance. Suddenly he smiled and came up to me.

"My name's Valter," he said.

"And I'm Hilda," I responded.

It's difficult to describe the excitement I felt during that first shared meal. Suddenly I was back among people who were calm, quiet, and well-mannered, who sat around the table together discussing and solving issues that had come up that day in an easy-going manner. They hardly mentioned the war: the farm's management and everyday glitches were the topics of concern.

When we sat down to eat, my head was still covered in a scarf. Mrs. Lochte asked me to remove it. I felt uncomfortable doing that but abided.

"Why is your hair so short?" Valter asked. Go tell this German child about Auschwitz! I told him I'd been very sick and it made my hair fall out.

But he had more questions. "When did you leave Garssen? How long were you there for? Where are your Mama and Papa? Why didn't your relatives look after you? Why did they let you travel on your own?" And on it went. I answered as safely as I could.

And now from Mr. Lochte. "What was your father's profession?" A carpenter, I answered. "How much did he earn?" I told him that he often worked in villages and, instead of payment, would receive food because, in the city people didn't have money to pay and food was hard to buy. Mr. Lochte nodded, confirming the truth of wartime. That was a last minute brainwave that saved me from slipping into an embarrassing situation.

Surviving clearly required being very skilled at improvisation. It was impossible to guess what the next question would be. Answers must be given right away, in as natural a manner as possible, so that my hosts wouldn't sense hesitation on my part.

One day Mr. Lochte drove into Garssen. When he returned, he told his wife and me that he'd met with the Burgermeister, who said he'd written to the Ministry of Defense and, once again, received the same answer: my father was missing. Mr. Lochte said he'd also help search for him. What choice did I have but to thank him?

Some forty Ukrainian laborers made up the Lochte farm's work force. "Since you're German," Mrs. Lochte said, "you'll live with us in our house as part of the family." So taken aback, I could barely thank them.

After dinner Mrs. Lochte took me to the upper floor and showed me the room that would be mine. It was sparkling clean and prettily furnished. The bed was made up with crisp, white embroidered sheets, pillows, and a woolen blanket. I was so overwhelmed that I could barely breathe. "Perhaps you should rest now. After all, you've had a long day and you're no doubt quite tired," Mrs. Lochte said kindly. She stepped out, closing the door gently behind her.

Gingerly lying down on the comfortable bed, I couldn't believe that it was mine. I closed my eyes and opened them again. Real or dream? Either way, I hoped it'd last until liberation.

My thoughts went to Sheindy. How was her first evening? What questions had she been asked? What answers had she come up with? First thing the next morning, I decided, I'd have to visit her to be sure our stories corresponded fully, and ensure we gave the same answers to our hosting families. I wanted to avoid a situation where her answers were different from mine. We must not get caught lying!

In Garssen we'd tried preparing for the kinds of questions we might be asked, but none of us could guess what else might come up and need a quick response. It's hard to maintain a lie alone, but even harder when the lies needed to be coordinated among three of us. Clearly we'd have to stay closely in touch to be sure we said the same thing.

The next morning I came downstairs early to help Mrs. Lochte with her chores in the kitchen. Suddenly the door flew open. A Ukrainian woman of about twenty stepped in, without a 'good morning' or even 'hello,' looking furious. Noticing me, she seemed very surprised, wondering what happened overnight and why I was doing jobs she would normally have, it seemed.

Mrs. Lochte explained that I was a German refugee and that, from now on, I'd help her in the kitchen and home, while the young woman would work in the fields with the other laborers. She was furious that, because of a German refugee, she'd now have to do fieldwork, collecting cabbages in the cold winter air.

It was dislike at first sight: from the moment she saw me and every time afterwards, the Ukrainian's eyes were daggers. If looks could kill she would have killed me, for sure. I knew right away that she was my number one enemy and I'd be well advised to keep as much distance from her as possible.

Going into the yard, I looked around at this pastoral village, at the smoke spiraling into the sky from homes' chimneys, and I stood there as though paralyzed, remembering the tongues of fire coming from the Auschwitz crematoria where the ovens of extermination burnt round the clock. I couldn't help but think about how, there, the fires were constantly fueled by the bodies of humans who'd first been horribly brutalized and tortured.

And I couldn't help wondering: what do these friendly people in their tranquil village know of the suffering experienced by prisoners in the concentration camps and forced labor camps? They'd probably never heard of Mengele, the Doctor of Evil, and his monstrous experiments. They most certainly had never heard of Muselmenn who, due to severe. long-term hunger, became walking skeletons. Crying was pointless, even risky here. I headed to the shed for firewood.

As soon as the opportunity arose, I ran through the fields to visit my sister. She and I had agreed-upon signs when we wanted to be alone. We walked into the yard. In undertones I told her what I'd been asked and the answers I'd given. Sheindy described her first night with her hosts. We exchanged information and decided to meet as often as possible to correlate our responses.

My integration into the family went well. The little boy, Valter, was friendly towards me and I was able to use him a lot to my advantage even though he had no idea what I was doing.

On one occasion, for instance, Mrs. Lochte asked me to bring rhubarb and some apples from the basement storage. I had no idea what rhubarb was but, as a good German girl, how could I admit that, especially when it turned out to be a very common item used in pies and compote. So I asked Valter if he'd like to help me. Down we went, and I suggested that he get the rhubarb while I chose the apples. I watched him closely, and took note of the illustration on the box, storing the information for next time.

There were numerous other occasions where resourcefulness helped me sidestep tricky situations. Although I seemed to be well-integrated into the family, I knew I had to be wary all the time. One wrong word and our secret would be discovered. So I chose to be a mostly quiet young woman, speaking only when spoken to, which was perfect: 'my family' simply thought my quietness was due to worry about my father on the front.

Adjusting to being part of a normal family whose lives had never been shaken up wasn't easy. The fact that I constantly needed to lie to my hosts upset me, especially because they fully believed me and had taken me in with open arms, giving me a warm home.

My fluency in German was already very good by the time I reached Ohe: it had improved because we'd been surrounded by it, spoken by the SS, the Kapos, the camp managers and block leaders, and so on. In the Greenberg weaving factory I'd worked alongside German civilians with whom I conversed in German. Slowly I'd become proficient. But I was still aware that I didn't speak with the same naturalness as a German. I had a lot yet to learn, and better sooner than later, I thought. When I was spoken to, I tried to use the speaker's words or phrases as far as possible in my answers. And I also tried to talk as much as possible with Valter, preferably out of everyone else's earshot, attempting to emulate his enunciation.

Between the first and second world wars, one could manage well without knowing German. Many schools taught German as a second language but, in Czechoslovakia, we studied Yiddish, Hungarian, Russian and Czech. German wasn't taught.

Sheindy and I were able to meet every day for brief snatches, the number of times we met directly linked to the number or type of questions we were asked that day. If either of us had needed to respond or explain something to our hosts that could endanger us, we'd immediately get together and hug tightly for a couple of minutes, long enough to whisper the update before quickly going back 'home.'

I once heard the two women talking about it. "How lovely it is," Mrs. Lochte said, "the way they hug each other for a few moments, kiss each other and run back to the house." They had no idea what the hug actually concealed.

Simultaneous to the cabbage collection season several cows, just having given birth, remained in the cowshed. All available hands were a blessing in the fields. That left Mrs. Lochte milking the cows on her own. One day she asked me about that.

"Hilda, do you know how to milk a cow?"

"Milk them?" I was taken by surprise and, at the same time, thinking that milking was the last thing I needed! But I quickly pulled myself together. "Do you have goats on the farm?" I asked her.

Now it was her turn to look amazed. "Goats? Why goats? We have cows."

Now that I knew there were no goats, I could go to the next step. "I know how to milk goats," I smiled at her.

"Well," Mrs. Lochte said, "if you can milk goats, then of course you can learn how to milk cows! It's almost the same thing."

And quickly I learned how to do it. It wasn't long before Mrs. Lochte would remain happily in her kitchen while I milked the cows three times a day. But, later that day, I heard her telling her husband that I'd asked about goats. It turned into a family joke.

Mr. Lochte was stocky and of average height. His hair was gray. His eyes, always expressing kindness, showed that he put great faith in people and was always willing to listen to others. Understanding him was a little complicated because several teeth were missing, making him slur parts of his words. He also had what sounded to me like a heavy German accent, which required me to pay close attention. Even if I hadn't asked him to repeat what he said, he often did. As odd as it sounded, I liked and respected my new patron.

In the evenings, when the family sat together in the living room listening to news on the radio, Mr. Lochte would explain its greater implications to the family, detailing the state of things 'at the front.'

There was a bomb shelter in the family's yard. Mr. Lochte instructed us pack food, water and first aid, as well as blankets in case anything happened and we needed to make use of it. The news in their sons' letters home were not optimistic. They were no longer conveying updating them about the German army's advance, but rather the evacuation of the wounded and the suffering the healthy were experiencing.

Listening to it all, my heart danced with joy. I would run to my sister, Margarete, the name I'd chosen for Sheindy when we arranged our papers at the Ministry of the Interior, and the name she was used to being called from her schooldays, shared these important bits of information with her, and then race back the Lochte's house. "Be patient," I'd tell Sheindy and our cousin, "our liberation is not far off."

THE COATS

Every concentration camp had its own method for marking prisoners to ensure they couldn't escape easily. In Auschwitz it was a top and pants with broad vertical stripes made from ash-gray cloth. In my sister's camp, the backs of coats were marked by a red vertical stripe. The young women, dressed in their coats, would line up and move forward one at a time so that a German with a can of red paint could stripe it from neck to hem. Where I was, a 15 x 15 centimeter square was cut out of the back. A patch of the same striped cloth as used in Auschwitz was inserted to fill the space.

It was the peak of winter and we couldn't simply get rid of our coats. Who knew what might happen or if we'd still need them? I had to figure a way to hide these brandings. When we traveled from Garssen to Celle. we wore the coats as-is, an extremely dangerous act. I found a solution for my coat by removing one of the external pockets and stitching it over the striped square.

As for Sheindy's coat, I tried various methods to remove it but failed miserably. I had no choice but to undo the stitches and sew it back up in a way that the red stripe would be unseen. First I removed the lining, then opened one seam and restitched it from its other side, continuing seam by seam. I knew that if I took the whole coat apart in one go I'd never get it back together again properly. Every evening after work I'd go to my sister and hand-stitch her coat.

Sometimes Mrs. Lochte would accompany me, chatting for

a while with her friend Mrs. Laupper, watching how the coat would come apart and then be resewn. Everything had to be hand stitched because we sisters didn't have a sewing machine, and I didn't have the gumption to ask Mrs. Lochte if I could borrow hers. Perhaps she thought I didn't know how to use one so never offered it.

Three weeks after starting the job, I finally sewed the buttons back on and my sister could wear her coat. Even our hosts were excited when I'd completed the work. We celebrated; most of all, I was pleased that my sister now had unmarked clothing.

Returning from Celle one day, our cousin said that she'd found work in one of the city hospitals and would be leaving the village. She gave us the address. The next day she left. Being older, our cousin had lived and eaten her meals with the Ukrainians and worked in the fields with them, which she didn't like at all. This, she explained to us, was her primary reason for leaving. But Sheindy was viewed as a German refugee and lived in the home with her host family, eating meals with them at their dining room table.

Over time, the tension in the atmosphere dropped noticeably and the questions stopped, which we found reassuring. Margarete-Sheindy tried to be busier than ever, making her unavailable to chat with anyone, especially with the Ukrainians who she did her utmost to avoid. The fact that she was 'German' infuriated them. But the arguments never ceased. She had to be constantly on guard around them. They'd arrived two years before us and felt they had set down roots. On one hand, they pitied my sister, who was still a girl but, on the other, she enjoyed preferential treatment and was prioritized by the hosting family, which angered them deeply.

Another problem also surfaced which I had to deal with: the number tattooed on my arm during my second stint at Auschwitz. How could I hide it from my hosts? There was only one way: to always wear long sleeves. In order to ensure I could never roll them up, or that no one could push them up, I hand-stitched the openings as narrow as feasible, and also put a bandage over the number, just in case. Should anyone notice the bandage, I'd just say I have a scratch.

Life took on a simple routine. Work, meals with the family, work and repeat. Nonetheless I was consumed with worry. Although I'd decided not to think about the past, about our home and parents, about our siblings, in moments of difficulty I couldn't help thinking of home. We had no photos of our parents, but their images were clearly engraved in my mind.

In my thoughts, I'd consult with my father, seeking his advice, conducting discussions or even arguments, presenting my case, knowing fully well that he would probably have suggested or decided differently.

I could hear him. "There's no logic to what you're doing."

And then I'd answer: "But Tateh, is this a logical time? Had I operated according to logic I wouldn't have reached this farm and this family!"

Some things aren't in our control. Circumstances can force us into illogical actions or drive us to bravely and brazenly take risks. Lying in bed at night, I would close my eyes and try to imagine my parents, not always succeeding yet attempting to talk to them. "Tateh, I'm sorry I have to live by lying, I'm sorry that I can't say a single word of truth. I know that's not how you raised us, but the day will come when you'll be proud of me!"

At the clinic, I handed Mrs. Lochte's note to her doctor. He prescribed medication and wrote down treatment instructions, as well as what to do if the rash reappeared. I thanked him. Sheindy and I left, deciding not to go back to the village right away but to stroll around for a while.

We looked for our people, Jews who'd fled from concentration camps and were in hiding in cities or villages nearby. We found one here, another there, always alone. Not once did we see them in twos or threes. They walked about quietly, heads down, yet very clearly paying close attention to their surroundings. I drew closer to a Jewish refugee, stopped in front of him, and began to talking in Yiddish. Because I no longer covered my hair, he could see that it was still clipped very short. He glanced at us before speaking.

"Where are you from?"

"Hungary," I answered.

"Hold on tight, liberation's close." Then he walked away without looking back or even saying goodbye. I was very moved, realizing that there could be any number of Jews hiding in Celle. Had they also jumped out of the same train we had?

These encounters encouraged and moved me. Every time my finger began hurting, I'd take Sheindy with me to the doctor in Celle. After treatment we'd walk around looking for fellow Jews. Sheindy's host family, the Lauppers, had an aunt living in Celle. Mrs. Redige would frequently visit the village so got to know us well. She was a pleasant, chit-chatty woman, a childless widow. Viewing herself as our aunt too, she would invite us to visit with her when we were in town.

On one of our forays into Celle we decided to pop in. She received us warmly and set up a table in the garden, serving coffee and cakes. Then she invited us inside. We sat in her living room and listened while she played a piano concerto for us! She asked us to come again, and gave us food to take back. We bid our goodbyes and began walking back to Ohe.

How absurd, I thought, for us two Jewish girls to escape the concentration camps, yet be hosted by this German woman who received us with the same courtesies and elegance of German culture as she'd welcome German friends or guests.

Over time, Sheindy and I received various items of clothing from our hostesses. Going to Celle gave us an opportunity to dress nicely. The good food we were enjoying and the village's fresh air were doing wonders for our health and well-being. Other than our still-quite-short hair, no one would have guessed we weren't German, and certainly would never have imagined that we were extermination camp escapees.

On one occasion while were in Celle, we heard raid sirens. We stood frozen where we were, not knowing where to go. A police officer standing nearby was shouting instructions. "Schnell!, Schnell!! To the bomb shelter!" With silent glances, Sheindy and I decided to run where everyone else was running.

The large public bomb shelter was well-organized for hundreds of people. Benches and chairs lined the walls. In a corner I noticed large containers of water, first aid packs, and fire extinguishers. The bomb shelter filled to capacity. We sat down on a bench tucked away near a corner and waited, hearing planes descending and dropping a series of bombs. That completely panicked me. How long would the air raid sirens continue? We needed to walk thirteen kilometers to the village. Terrified and tense, we could do nothing but remain in the shelter.

An older woman was sitting next to me. She started a conversation: where we were from, what were we doing in the city, where were our parents, why hadn't they come to fetch us? She warned us of how dangerous it was for two youngsters to be wandering about alone unsupervised and begged us to promise that, as soon as the shelter let everyone out, we'd go home as fast as we could. Of course, we promised.

The woman began explaining to others on the bench that we'd come from one of the nearby villages, the name of which we purposely hadn't specified, and that we'd found ourselves in the shelter by chance. Suddenly she opened her bag, took out sandwiches and gave them to us. "You must be starving," she smiled. We felt embarrassed but nonetheless thanked her.

The phrase 'if the shoe fits, wear it' was very apt right then. We felt like we were cheating, but realized that no one suspected a thing, even though it seemed to us that everyone was gazing at us.

A tall, bespectacled man sat opposite me, a large leather bag lying across his knees. He took a notepad from it and began writing. Every so often he looked up. Was he staring at me? I was horrified. Did I look suspicious? Was the word 'Jew' emblazoned on my forehead? Would he call the police? Or was he a journalist writing about the Allied Forces' air raid on Celle and I held no interest for him? The release bell sounded. Everyone could leave. We did too, as quickly as we could.

The roar of tanks was already clearly heard in Ohe. Initially, it was more muffled but grew consistently louder, making me excited and even joyful. But of course I couldn't display such emotions to my adoptive household and, instead, had to pretend to be scared. To me, though, the booms coming from the Allies' tanks were like the calls announcing the Messiah. The sound of shots was also growing by the day. I began allowing myself to hope that liberation was truly at hand and that the wars' end was clearly on the horizon. Perhaps soon we'd be free at last?

Speaking with Sheindy away from prying eyes and ears, we noted how Germany's fall seemed imminent. We knew it was still far too early to rejoice, but at least we could now see the light at the end of the tunnel. German residents were extremely fearful but our happiness grew. Liberation was coming! Slowly, yes, but it would eventually arrive!

On one of our visits to Celle, we decided to visit our cousin at her new workplace. The hospital reception clerk sent us to the head nurse, a tall aggressive woman who interrogated us.

"Who are you?"

I explained that we're Mali's sisters.

"Not possible," she said, "Mali is Polish and you're German."

Oh dear, I thought, we've had it now. Had Mali said she's Polish? Maybe she never said a word about us. Maybe she got herself into trouble with her story? Could she no longer be at the hospital? Had she changed jobs without telling us?

Possibilities raced through my mind as the head nurse glared at us sharply, suspicious, asking us more and more questions. Suddenly a woman cradling an infant hurt in a traffic accident near the hospital ran into the hospital, screaming hysterically for help. The head nurse told us to wait a few moments, saying she'd be right back. The instant she led the woman into a different room and closed the door behind them, we left, passing through the large waiting room, praying that the head nurse wouldn't catch us. The second we crossed the yard, we ran off, too scared to look behind us. For as long as the Germans maintained control, we never went back to the hospital.

IT'S CHRISTMAS!

Christmas was approaching. The mood in the Laupper and Lochte homes was increasingly festive. Mrs. Lochte said that she'd love it if the family, me included, would attend church together. I was given a pretty outfit and given new shoes. *That's all I need*, I kept thinking. The very idea that I would be stepping into a church sickened me.

At the first opportunity, I ran to Sheindy, telling her of the family's plans. Maybe together we could figure a way for me to get out of it. We decided to do everything in our power not to go worshipping with the family.

Christmas Eve arrived. The turkey was cooking in the oven, cakes were baked, scents from the kitchen drove everyone crazy. We were all dressed, looking tiptop, ready to go. Harnessed to two horses, the wagon stood at the ready in the yard.

Again and again Mrs. Lochte checked that everything was ready for the feast, which included many different courses. The meal was also planned for the 35 to 40 Ukrainian laborers. The young Ukrainian woman was meant to fetch the pots and take them to the laborers' dining hall, but Mrs. Lochte didn't completely trust her. She insisted that, on this festival, the laborers would receive what she'd cooked directly from her.

I predicted that this problem would crop up. It matched my plans perfectly. Patiently I waited until Mrs. Lochte raised the matter herself. She suggested we all go together to church and she'd join us later, after serving the laborers. Speaking softly, I suggested that maybe 'this time' I could forego church and stay here so that she could join her family. I also suggested that next time she could make it up to me. My idea was warmly embraced. So was I. Mrs. Lochte thanked me numerous times for being willing to stay home instead of her.

On Christmas Day my sister came running over, pale and trembling. She discovered that her host, Mr. Laupper, was a policeman! And not just any ordinary policeman, but the district officer, which she only learned because he was decked out in full uniform in honor of Christmas. I was stunned. Up until that day we had no idea that Sheindy was living in the home of a German closely linked to the law. *Oh dear*, my thoughts went, *is this Santa's surprise for Sheindy and me?* But after calming down a little and thinking rationally, I told Sheindy there was nothing we could do about it now except keep acting normally. Our confidence sunk and we were filled with greater worry.

Guests came to visit the Lochtes on Christmas Day. By arrangement, I was to serve the coffee and cake. I prepared everything on a tray and went to the pantry for the cake. There were two beautiful large cakes, one with apples and the other with cherries. What a delight for eye and palate! The cherry cake appealed to me more, so I started cutting slices and arranging them on plates. Mrs. Lochte suddenly came into the kitchen, saying that she wanted to serve the apple cake.

She began putting the slices I'd already cut back into the cake tray when she suddenly realized one piece was missing. Yes, my craving had gotten the better of me and I'd eaten from the cake before anyone else had tasted it! Mrs. Lochte didn't say anything. She just smiled at me, while my face burned with shame. I swore to myself that I'd never be tempted to do something like that again. During my entire stay there I had access to the Lochte household's home and pantry but I never took advantage of their trust, other than that one slice of cherry cake.

Two months passed. Sheindy and I still lived with our host

families in Ohe. The rumblings and booms from tanks grew closer and louder. For me it was reassuring background music. For the Germans it was the sound of approaching doom. Dozens of jets flew overhead. People talked endlessly of the great blitz which the Allies would soon rain down on them. I dreamt of the war's end.

Every day that passed was a blessing from Sheindy's and my perspective. Every day also increased our jumpiness, especially since I sat with the family in the evenings listening to the radio's news broadcasts.

My birthday was in January. Mrs. Lochte decided we needed to celebrate, preparing a wonderful cake and buying a small gift: a blouse with long sleeves. How lucky that my birthday was in winter! Mr. Lochte congratulated me and little Valter drew a bouquet of flowers in a multitude of colors. My special day was also marked by a half day off. Sheindy baked sesame and honey biscuits. It felt so odd to be congratulated and pampered. I'd never even imagined such kindness during this war.

One day a letter arrived from the Ministry of Defense. For a moment I was terrified but, once again, it provided the same news: my father was missing. Mr. Lochte tried to raise my spirits and promised he'd never stop searching: it was surely just a matter of time before he'd be found. What could I say? He was so well-meaning, but I hoped and prayed he'd never succeed. When the second Ministry of Defense letter showed up, advising that he was still viewed as missing, I allowed myself some moments of true sorrow, and cried freely.

But the next time I met up with Sheindy, I told her how concerned I was over Mr. Lochte's dedication to his goal, which could end up being a catastrophe for us. We were stuck: I couldn't say a word or make any remarks. I had to accept the situation naturally and show gratitude for their perseverance.

One day Valter suggested we go riding the horses. I flatly refused, saying that I didn't know how, which was the truth this time, and added that I was deathly scared to mount the horse, which was also true. But Valter wasn't giving up so easily, I ran out of excuses, and found myself riding a horse.

My heart pounded with fear and uncertainty. Valter rode the other horse alongside me, not trying to make me go faster. We rode very, very slowly for several days until I began to feel more comfortable until, several days later, I emulated Valter, pressed my heels against the horse and started galloping like the wind. But I didn't know how to stop the horse!

Valter, catching on to the situation immediately, rode faster, passed me, and wheeled around to face the horse I was riding in an effort to halt it. But my horse took fright, rose up on its hind legs, and I could feel myself between heaven and earth. I held onto those reins as though my life depended on it until the horse slowly calmed down. But I was grateful to Valter for this experience. I learned to ride, and we had some fun times together.

Sunday was a day of rest. The Ukrainian laborers would hold parties, play the accordion, dance, sing, and enjoy themselves. They also invited Ukrainians from other farms to join them. Mrs. Lochte suggested every so often that I join them, dancing, having a nice time, but I refused, each time coming up with a new excuse. I wanted to avoid being among them at all costs.

These laborers spoke a version of Ukrainian which was very similar to Ruthenian, an Eastern Slavic language, so I was able to understand almost everything they said, but was afraid they'd realize I could comprehend and think me insolent for not answering their questions. Better to keep a healthy distance and stay in Mrs. Lochte's house, especially since on one occasion, when I'd overhead them talking about Mrs. Lochte and I instinctively made a movement as though readying to answer and come out in her defense. At the very last second, I held back.

But the Ukrainian young woman had caught me out. "I think that girl knows what we're saying!" she told the others. I was between a rock and a hard place, so told them that I'd managed to learn a few words of Ukrainian since coming to Ohe. Clearly, though, they didn't buy my explanation and remained suspicious.

Longing for my parents, my family and home very pronouncedly surfaced one day. I desperately needed to see them, to hear their voices. Going into my bedroom, I pulled out the lapel with the emblem that I'd cut from Tateh's jacket in Greenberg. For the first time during these long months of tension and acting a certain persona I burst into tears and gave my emotions free rein. Would I ever see any of my family again? Would any of them return from the horrors of the concentration camps?

An answer to my prayers came in the roar and thunder of tanks that drew me out of my sorrow. *Yes, there's hope*, I reminded myself. *Liberation was near. A bit longer. I need to hold on a bit longer.* How often I'd repeated that phrase in my mind! I presumed my parents had perished in Auschwitz but, as I hadn't actually seen their bodies, buried them, nor sat 'shiva,' the seven days of mourning according to Jewish custom, somewhere in my subconscious there was still hope that they'd miraculously return home.

THE ADOPTION PROPOSAL

Sitting with my host family one evening, chatting about problems on the farm resulting from the war, Mr. and Mrs. Lochte discussed how the Ukrainian laborers were openly talking about the moment that the Allied Forces would liberate them, leaving them free to go wherever they wished.

The atmosphere was pleasant and I felt comfortable in the Lochte household. Mrs. Lochte mentioned that I'd integrated so well into their family that it felt as though I'd been with them for years. She added how sorry she was that my mother had passed away and my father was missing. She also noted how close she'd become to me and that she, her husband, and Valter loved me very much.

And then, the bombshell. They had no daughters, only boys, and... they would love to legally adopt me! And then they gazed at me expectantly.

I was stunned, not able to believe what I'd heard. Adopt me? I was still a minor, but felt myself so mature and responsible. I had to be extremely careful now about every word I chose even though, deep in my heart, I was cheering for myself at being victorious over the Germans! But their proposal caught me off guard and I needed to buy some time to think and conscientiously form my response.

The Lochtes really were wonderful people and I didn't want to hurt them, but what should I say? They talked on about they had been planning a visit to the Ministry of the Interior in Celle, to 'arrange all the papers.' I really was moved by their offer. Eventually I pulled myself together, thanking them for their trust, but explained that I first needed to talk to my sister. They agreed.

Meeting up with Sheindy the next morning, we talked about the 'generous offer' and contemplated how to deal with it. One thing was certain: whether I agreed or not, things had now gotten extremely complex for me. The issue was understanding which option was less risky. On one hand, I didn't want to hurt them. On the other, I feared that carrying out a formal adoption could bring a multitude of complexities to the fore. The government offices may want to unearth my birth certificate, investigate my past, or ask for identifying addresses, names of relatives and various details. Countless scenarios ran through my mind.

The best option, it seemed, would be to agree in principle, but ask that the adoption be postponed until after the war was over. I felt like I was between a rock and a hard place. Again the more worrisome thoughts surfaced: were they harboring suspicions and was their way of verifying them?

Sheindy and I decided that I'd agree to becoming their adopted daughter. Grinning from ear to ear, I told Mrs. Lochte that I'd be very happy to join the family. Little Valter danced around, whooped with joy, and kissed each of my cheeks. Mr. and Mrs. Lochte hugged me tight. What joy in the house! And I kept thinking: just let time take its course and we'll see how the matter plays out.

What would my status now be in the household as their 'daughter?' I wondered about it momentarily but didn't give it much more thought. How absurd, I thought, that their sons are in the Third Reich army trying to eradicate my people, that tanks and warplanes were moving in on us, but Mrs. Lochte is focused on one thing: adoption papers. It suddenly turned into the most important aspect of her life, almost as though she feared I'd try to run away.

I let some days pass, trying not to think about the matter any further. I can't do very much to change the situation, I could only hope the outcome would be good.

The day came. Mrs. Lochte decided the family would travel together to Celle. She brought out documents, certificates, filled in forms, wrote, signed, barely asked me anything. Trembling and pale, I watched. She was sure I was showing signs of excitement.

When we left their home, I was Hilda Herscowitz. When we returned, I was Hilda Lochte, adopted daughter of a German family! How would I refer to Mrs. Lochte now? Mama? Or by her personal name? Once again, I thought it best to say nothing and wait to see how that would work itself out. Meanwhile, I wouldn't use any title (although in this memoir, I'll continue calling her Mrs. Lochte).

Mrs. Lochte wrote to both her sons, who'd already heard about me from previous correspondence, and updated them in great detail about the adoption. The fact that her sons were serving was deeply concerning. What awaited me when they returned home and the truth would eventually come to light? They'd kill me, of that I was certain. They would say I made a mockery of their war. The country had finally rid itself of its Jews, and here was this one who'd slipped between the cracks and not only survived, but became part of their family!

Shortly after the adoption, Mrs. Lochte asked me to call her by her given name. So sometimes I called her Helga or Ida, I truly can't remember which, and sometimes Mrs. Lochte. She didn't seem to mind and didn't make a fuss of it. But I continued calling her husband 'Mr. Lochte.'

Life carried on smoothly until, one evening, Mr. Laupper showed up, rifle in hand. *Uh-oh,* was my first thought. *Not good.* Was he here in his official capacity as the district officer? I knew he only had the rifle with him when something had gone wrong in the village.

Mr. Laupper looked straight at Mr. Lochte. "We found two Jews in the village!" I thought I was going to faint. I didn't dare look up. I began to sweat. I kept thinking the worst: Sheindy must have said something that had now trapped us.

How many thoughts raced through my mind in those moments? The tension coursed through my body. Had they arrested my sister? Were her wrists and ankles chained? Was she being guarded to prevent her escape? I wanted to scream. I wanted to dash over there and see she was alright.

A short pause later which, to me, seemed like eons, he said more specifically, "I found two Jewish men in the village." Only then I dared raise my head. Mrs. Lochte had noticed, though. "Oh dear, look," she said to Mr. Laupper, "Hilda's so worked up about it that she's on the verge of fainting!" She brought me water, hugged me, and spoke soothing words. But at least now I knew Sheindy was safe, that neither of us were in imminent danger.

In one of the cowsheds, Ukrainian laborers had found two prisoners in their striped uniforms, numbers marked on the upper left side of the shirt, as was customary in concentration camps. The prisoners said they'd fled a forced labor camp and asked to be kept hidden until liberation. Although the Ukrainians had no idea what a concentration camp or forced labor camp was, they decided to hide them in the cowshed, set up a place for them to sleep, and bring them blankets, water and food. But some days later, matters began to get complicated. The laborers decided to tell the Ukrainian foreman, who lived on the Laupper's farm, about the situation. Having no other choice, the foreman then informed the district officer.

From that point on, it went from snowball to avalanche. That same evening Mr. Laupper, as district officer, went to see the prisoners. He brought them out after handcuffing them and began interrogating them, but when the prisoners said that the SS in Auschwitz was exterminating Jews, whether men, women, children or elderly, Mr. Laupper didn't believe them. Clearly this German village was so isolated, they had absolutely no concept of concentration camps, nor had they heard of a place called Auschwitz.

Mrs. Laupper prepared food for them but was afraid to take it to them. Despite the prisoners bearing no weapons, people were afraid to approach them. And that's why Sheindy volunteered to take them the tray of food, and set out to help the two pitiful men. She knew exactly what they were going through.

Mr. Laupper and others decided that they had no choice but to bring the prisoners to the Celle police. As it turned out, the next day my sister and I were also supposed to be traveling to the doctor in Celle to renew the rash cream prescription. Who was in the milk wagon that day? Two Jewish male prisoners, a German guard, and two Jewish 'German' girls.

The sun had barely begun lighting the day. Birds chirped, which lifted my spirits a bit. Of course the prisoners thought we were German. In their efforts to prevent us from understanding, they spoke to each other in Hungarian! I saw them gazing at the sandwiches I'd packed for Sheindy's and my day out, but they didn't dare request them. When we reached the city, I gave them the package: sandwiches, fruit and cake. Sheindy and I hopped down from the wagon and went on our way without saying a word the entire time.

Shortly afterwards, investigators from Celle came to the farm, collecting evidence from the village's foreign laborers. They wanted to know the location of the place that the two Jews said they'd fled, and why they'd chosen this particular village. What incredible tension. The investigators didn't believe a word that the prisoners said when it came to details about concentration camps, nor did they believe that they'd randomly reached Ohe. They were also skeptical of the laborers, who denied all connection with the prisoners, explaining that they'd merely given them food and shelter.

The investigation dragged on and on, its end nowhere in sight. The village was in a state of fluster and work wasn't progressing at all. During that period I met up with my sister several times a day to coordinate our answers should we somehow get called on and questioned. We were both terribly afraid.

Then the investigators showed up at our farm. I tried to stay calm but, when I saw the men coming down the pathway towards the house, my knees turned to jelly. I kept reassuring myself, going over answers in my mind, but I knew that there could always be a surprise question which would require me to think on the spot and come up with a quick answer to avert any doubt.

First on the list were Mr. and Mrs. Lochte, who were asked if they'd seen any suspicious movements or activities on the farm, or odd behaviors among their foreign workers. Mr. Lochte said he hadn't noticed a thing. Mrs. Lochte said the same. Then the investigator called on me. Once again, my life story was rolled out: a German refugee, although I didn't say where from, my father was a German soldier considered MIA. Commiserating with me, the investigator said that the war would probably soon be over, and Germany would be victorious. "Don't worry about your father," he said gently, "he'll almost certainly return alive and well."

Seated at the kitchen table with the Lochtes, the investigators chatted about how their questioning was progressing. I kept my mouth tightly shut: one wrong word and I'd be as good as dead. They spoke about a train carrying Jewish prisoners that had passed several months ago through Celle and that several had attempted to escape. All had been caught except for four females who disappeared with no sign of them. When he'd been called to Ohe, he wondered if the four prisoners had been found.

Why is he mentioning this, I couldn't help wondering. Was he alluding to something? Did he suspect me? Or was this no more than postulating and idle small talk while drinking coffee? I was so scared that I lost my voice and couldn't speak, thinking of the number on my arm which, although covered by a bandage, could easily be made visible. Again, I broke out in a cold sweat.

The investigator must have sensed my discomfort, turning to me. "You've got nothing to worry about," he said warmly. "I'm only questioning the foreign workers, and you're a German refugee." How Sheindy and I breathed with relief once they'd left the village and routine was restored!

Spring came, the earth became green again, shoots and buds and blossoms bursting forth, trees leafing up. After the long snowy winter, I truly enjoyed the sun's warmth. Not far from Ohe was a stream where villagers and laborers would swim, and farm owners and their laborers from the nearby regions would get together. One day Valter asked me to go swimming with him. My dreaded fear! I knew I'd have to face this head-on one day, and I also knew I'd never go swimming. No one could ever see that number on my arm. Bandage or not, I didn't want to take any chances and so looked for a good excuse to stay home.

My insistence on not going annoyed him but I couldn't give in, no matter how nice I wanted to be to him. Valter told his father that I refused to take him swimming. Luckily, Mr. Lochte was a very decent fellow. "If Hilda doesn't want to go, there must be a very good reason; we need to respect her wishes, otherwise she wouldn't refuse so persistently." That made me feel really bad but the stream, as far as I was concerned, was my newest number one enemy.

The warmer the weather became, the harder it got to hide the tattoo. I'd narrowed the cuffs on my clothes so that they couldn't ride higher than a few centimeters above my wrist, keeping the tattoo a secret. It was unpleasant to constantly walk around with long sleeves which, in light of the seasonal change, introduced a new array of questions and answers.

On a warm spring day, Mrs. Lochte asked me why I didn't roll my sleeves up. "It'd be much more comfortable if you had short sleeves." Her tone was somewhere between statement and suggestion. So I had to come up with a plausible reason. "When I was little," I explained, "I'd been very sick with (and now I can't remember the name of the diseases I mentioned). Although I'm healthy now, the result was that I really suffer from the cold and have to stay well-dressed. Long-sleeved dresses or tops are a must for me."

Mrs. Lochte cocked her head slightly, listening intently, then responded by saying that perhaps it could be treated. Could it be from negligence due to the war? She would take me to her doctor. I truly appreciated her concern but kept insisting that I absolutely wanted to continue wearing long sleeves. I could see how my obstinance took her a little by surprise. She wasn't used to that kind of response from me because I'd always done my best to be compliant, obedient, surrendering to her lead. She found my refusal to see the doctor strange.

The next day, Mrs. Lochte brought me a short sleeved dress. She was quite shocked when I refused to try it on. I did promise, though, that if I felt long sleeves were getting too uncomfortable for me I'd definitely wear the dress. She didn't raise the subject again after that. She waited patiently for the summer to hit full force.

The tanks' rumble and roar had now become a fundamental part of our lives. Work carried on but, for Sheindy and me, every shot that rang out was a harbinger of freedom. When liberation seemed to be at our fingertips, a telegram arrived from Günter, the family's younger soldier, advising that he'd been injured and was on his way home. His close friend, also injured, would be accompanying him.

Every day brought some new surprise. Every revelation raised some new problem. Real problems! Not only was their son returning, but bringing an injured friend with him to recuperate. Once again I'd be questioned, once again I'd have to think on my feet when answering unexpected inquiries.

And they probably wouldn't let me off with superficial answers. They'd probably badger me half to death. Two soldiers on sick leave at home would have plenty of time to make things really tough for me, even if they didn't mean to: after all, for them it'd be no more than getting to know me. For me, it would be nerve-wracking angst. In my heart, I was so sorry my 'brother' was returning. If only he could have remained where he was, at the glorious front! Meanwhile we readied the house for two soldiers. We had no idea what their injuries actually were, or how the injuries might affect their behavior and needs.

Another telegram came to the house specifying their arrival date. The family was very excited, but the absence of clear information on their injuries put a damper on their happiness.

The great day came. A car drove into the yard. The family ran out to receive the two young men. I stayed inside, but peeked out through the window. I saw two young men get out of the car and walk, unaided: no one from the family supporting them, no walking stick, no crutches. Clearly they weren't in such a terrible state.

What excitement when they walked inside! Valter couldn't stop pestering them, asking incessant questions. Not wanting to butt in on the intimate family reunion, I busied myself, waiting until the mood calmed down a little. Certain that at some point they'd start talking about me, it would be easier for me, and them, if I wasn't present. Not too long later Valter found me, asking me to join the family in the guest room.

My mind was dizzy with thoughts. I felt as though I was facing a firing squad. *Stay calm,* I kept telling myself, *be careful what you say.* I was sure that while the family had sat together without me, they'd told the boys my story. Or so I hoped. Walking in, they gazed at me, smiling. Günter was eventually the first to break the silence.

"When I left, we were three boys. Now here I am back home, and I've got a sister! Welcome! I hope you'll feel great among us here."

Their faces were a blur. All I could see were the uniforms, the hat, the gleaming boots, and I felt myself shudder.

We were formally introduced and then the questions began. Two young men against one younger me. My answers were as brief as I could make them without being offensive. And I kept reminding myself: *stay calm.*

Günter repeated how pleased he was to have a sister in the family and that he hoped we'd become good friends. I tried to change the subject as a way of halting what, to me, was starting to feel like an interrogation. It was too much for a first meeting, so I asked where and how he was injured. And I did manage to change the focus. He never even noticed as he started describing how he and his friend were wounded at the front, where he was hit in the shoulder and transported to hospital.

While recuperating, he learned that his friend had also been wounded and was in the same hospital. An order came one day to evacuate the hospital because the army 'needed to withdraw from its current position.' The two young men were returned to their battalion but it was in disarray, everyone fearing the advancing enemy. The two of them looked for their platoon but couldn't find it so, without giving it a second thought, slung their kitbags over their shoulders, didn't inform anyone, and simply fled. And now, of course, they'd be considered deserters.

Guntar went on and on, but my thoughts were already branching into different directions and I wasn't really listening anymore. Once again I was reminding myself: *hold on a bit longer, the war's almost over, it can't go on much more.* The Allied Forces were approaching in coordinated advances and no one would be able to stop them. Quietly I left the family group after bidding them all goodnight and wishing Guntar and his friend a speedy recovery and telling him how happy I am that he's home. And I went to my room.

My emotions were in too much turmoil to allow sleep. Thoughts, thoughts. Which army would enter this region of Germany? Americans? Brits? Russians? Whoever was destined to come, how long would it take? A week? Two? A month?

Not long after being brought to the Lochte family, I found a tiny music box in a corner of my room. Turning the miniature crank made the music box play a wonderful melody which always put me more at ease. I turned the handle now. So much had changed in the village. The tension was palpable.

The Ukrainian laborers brought here against their will and made to work in the farms spoke a lot about the developing situation. They'd meet up with other Ukrainians, sharing the latest news, recalculating the Red Army's moves, and surmising that it was already in the region. The laborers got edgy and less obedient, no longer fearing their 'employers' and began taking advantage of their situation.

One morning the tanks roared so loudly that it sounded as though they'd parked on the other side of the street. Hundreds of jets filled the skies, leaving long trails of fire. The noise was deafening. We raced to the bomb shelters. Only I stayed alone in the house, giving my standard excuse: someone had to stay here so that the Ukrainians wouldn't steal or loot.

How could I possibly stay with them in the bomb shelter at a time like this? I knew I'd never be able to hide my joy. For me, after all, the Allied Forces' jets were nothing but the most welcome news. We'd waited so long for this moment! In the concentration camps we waited for a sign, wanting to know if anyone cared about us, and now that time had come. I was sorry for everyone who didn't make it this far, but I was thrilled to know that something was being done to help those few of us who had survived.

I would have loved to run over to my sister, to share the happiness. How difficult it was to keep it to myself!

Although I'd been told it was absolutely forbidden, I stood at the window. I didn't want to miss a moment of this amazing sight. Dog fights in the sky! Planes exploding, burning like firebrands as they plunged down. I saw soldiers parachuting out. The flames looked far away, yet painted the sky scarlet. It felt like the planes were right above my head, like the end of the world had come.

Doors in the house ripped off their hinges, windows rattled, panes of glass shattered, objects were blasted across rooms. Would the house collapse on me? An ear-splitting explosion... Distancing from the window, I sat on a chair, breathless, waiting, waiting for the end of this attack and the sirens freeing everyone from the bunkers.

When the family returned they found me seated, pale, and shaking. I couldn't say a thing, as though my tongue had been lost. I was gently laid out on a bed. It took some time for me to calm down. Mrs. Lochte said that next time the air raid siren sounded, I'd go down with everyone to safety. She would not allow me to stay alone in the house anymore.

Often I wondered if fate wasn't playing games with me. Liberation was so close, but risks lurked in every corner. One day Günter's soldier friend, grinning, came to talk to me. Mrs. Lochte had mentioned to him that my family came from Guben. "Well! We lived not so far from each other!" he said, saying that he'd been born in Bender which, as far as I remembered, was very close to Guben. My brain went on high alert.

Why did we say we were from Guben? When we fled the train and reached the village we had to find a feasible cover story. We chose Guben as our birthplace because Sheindy worked in the weapons factory in Guben, which they'd reach on foot. She was a little familiar with the city, and had heard some details about it from the German civilians working alongside her.

We knew that numerous weapons factories were located in Guben, as well as factories producing men's and women's hats. We found out that it was well-known for its pretty parks and gardens filled with flowers of every color imaginable. We didn't know a whole lot about Guben, but we banked on the fact that the German families hosting us would know even less than us. And indeed we were in luck with that. The soldier told me that he knew the city well because he'd go there for shopping and entertainment, or to walk around the beautiful parks.

And suddenly he asked outright where we'd lived in Guben. From his descriptions, I understood where Bender was located, so I answered that we lived in a different, far more distanced part of the city. He mentioned cinemas, films and shows he'd seen. I said that I was too young to go alone to such places. Then he went on to mention various events occurring in the city. I pretended to remember bits and pieces. He mentioned the names of families there. I said that of course I didn't know them all, only some and only by name.

Among the names was that of a wealthy family. He grinned when he said what a privilege it had been to go out with their daughter before his enlistment. Did I know them? My answer: "They had such a lovely garden in front of the house." When he asked about another family, I replied that "they lived not too far from the park." That's how I managed to maneuver through the conversation. Günter's friend was thrilled. And I was happy that the conversation hadn't taken place at the family's dining room table where more people present might have given rise to even more questions.

Both soldiers were healing from their wounds, but they had no plans to return to the army. They cut off all contact with their battalion and instead spent their time listening to the news and analyzing the political situation in Germany. They'd argue heatedly if anyone cast doubt on the German army's ability to win. The news was primarily reporting defeats and withdrawals, but the two soldiers insisted that the army would come out of it just fine. They had also gone to town to collect news from battles on the frontlines; despite the news being bad for Germany, they believed that Germany would be victorious. Their blind faith verged on lunacy. Even Mrs. Lochte had noticed it, but explained it away as a possible impairment stemming from their injuries. Günter and his friend lived in constant fear of being caught and labeled AWOL, apprehensive that the military police could be searching for them. Too scared to go to the military commander's office in Celle, they decided to simply stay home and wait. They never spoke about Hitler. Nor did they mention concentration camps: as if they'd never heard of them.

One day Günter suggested I go with him to the city to celebrate having become part of the family. There wasn't any excuse I could come up with that made him leave me alone. Eventually I pulled out my life-saver: Mrs. Lochte, who pretty much always backed me up. But not this time. She thought it was a wonderful idea, especially if I would use this opportunity to buy some new clothes. My heart was screaming a warning. Only a miracle could save me from this trip.

On Saturday, there was a massive tank attack. Three times the air raid sirens sent us down to the bunkers. Another aerial dog-fight. In the evening, a long convoy of military vehicles and German soldiers reached the village. Clearly the German army was withdrawing from our region too. The overthrow must be soon! I could have danced with joy, but I knew better than to show any sign of emotion. I dashed over to Sheindy. In her room we hugged and kissed, bouncing up and down on our toes so as to make no noise. To literally jump for joy would have been dreadfully dangerous. A little longer! Not long now and we'll be free, we reminded each other.

The next morning Mr. Laupper came over to Mr. Lochte. They huddled in conversation for a lengthy period. He was extremely agitated and didn't go out to work his fields, but didn't feel solace at home either.

Mr. Lochte pulled Günter aside and recommended that the trip to town be postponed due to the newly developing situation. Thanks to Mr. Lochte, I was saved.

By now it was almost impossible to control the Ukrainian laborers. They didn't want to work, wouldn't listen to their supervisors and, although they had no radio, managed to pick up on the rumors flying around. They were certain that the Russian soldiers would liberate them and spoke about looting once the Russians arrived. Although I understood every word they said, I couldn't risk exposing Sheindy and me by warning Mrs. Lochte, for whom I was a German girl unfamiliar with the Ukrainian language.

But one day the young Ukrainian woman who'd worked in the kitchen before my arrival blurted the Ukrainians' intent right in Mrs. Lochte's face. She was crass and very aggressive. "When the Russians come they'll give us all your valuables, all the nice things in your house. They'll send you to Siberia. You're German, you're finished, kaput!" she said with loathing in her voice.

In fact, the Germans feared the Russians more than other Allied Forces. Mrs. Lochte was left in stunned silence at this outburst. She and Mr. Lochte spoke together, then began packing up their more valuable belongings, their better quality clothes and linens, tablecloths and dishes, boots and other items. They brought crates into the house one evening and I helped them pack.

During my stay with the family I'd put together a small collection of clothing. For Christmas I'd been given new shoes and a pretty top for church on Sundays. On some other occasion I'd received a dress and skirt. I never wore these items but believed they'd be useful after our liberation, when at last I could remove the bandage covering my arm tattoo without fear.

In her keenness to do right by everyone in the family, Mrs. Lochte asked me to bring my bundle of belongings too. I tried to persuade her it wasn't necessary, but nothing I said helped. The Ukrainian woman's threats had deeply shaken her. I ended up bundling my things together and she placed them into the family crate. That night the crates, my clothes also inside, were buried for safekeeping in German soil.

The further the Germans withdrew, the more the village filled with soldiers. They were everywhere: in courtyards and gardens, causing disarray and filth. Farmers fumed that their gardens and crops were being ruined but bit their tongues and said nothing. Officers walked freely in and out of homes, coming for a hot meal or coffee, or to chat with the families. Mrs. Lochte would present me as a German refugee, telling them that my father was a missing soldier for a long time now. That always earned their respect.

But I shook in my boots every time a German officer entered the house. Their familiar hats. Those crisply ironed uniforms. And, worst of all, the mirror-shine boots. It made my skin goosebump in fear. Those were the boots that kicked and trampled Jews in the camps. Those were the boots that killed Jewish babies by stomping on their heads, Those were the boots that clicked to attention. A nightmare that kept replaying in my head again and again.

THE THIRD REICH ARMY IN RETREAT

Visiting Sheindy one day, we whispered about the new situation shaping in the village due to the army's retreat. Sheindy was extremely anxious and feared that Mrs. Laupper might sense she was behaving differently. Sheindy's job in this new set of circumstances was to open the door to visitors, take their hats and coats and hang them up. She told me how German officers would pinch her rosy cheeks in an overly friendly manner as they walked in. "That's what a good German girl looks like!" they'd laugh, "blond hair, blue eyes, pink cheeks, always pleasant and friendly." Sheindy's heart would leap each time.

It took some time but the soldiers eventually left Ohe. Life went back to normal, more or less, and the village seemed to breathe a sigh of relief. It was nothing but the quiet before the storm.

Sheindy and I decided on a trip to Celle. Often we'd walk around there, hoping to meet other Jewish refugees, but generally that didn't happen. Once the snow melted we'd return via the forest, where we felt safe, and often broke into song, or spoke normally rather than in whispers as we did in the village. It was just us and the trees, birds tweeting overhead, and now the spring's flowers beginning to bud. We sang in Hungarian, which suddenly sounded so odd to us.

Crossing my fingers behind my back one day, I told Mrs. Lochte that I needed to go into Celle to see the doctor, because

I thought I had an infection. I must say that, of all my trips to the doctor, I only actually went to the clinic once! Once again Mrs. Lochte strongly encouraged me to buy clothes in town. She wanted to pamper me, but I didn't give her half a chance.

"We don't want to hang around there for too long. I'll go to the doctor and come right back home. Let's do shopping once things are quieter and more pleasant," I said. Once again I was saved from the short-sleeves shopping outing.

This time we didn't see a single Jewish refugee. We went up and down Celle's street, but we didn't see anyone. We returned to Ohe quite disappointed.

SHEINDY'S BIRTHDAY

My sister's birthday was at the end of March, and I decided to make her a small party. For a gift, she asked me to buy a harmonica. I thought it a little strange, but wanting to buy her something that would make her happy, I began to wonder how to find one. The war was still raging, life on the farm was still upside down, several times a day we dashed to the bomb shelters, and the Ukrainian workers could taste freedom in the air. The thunder of tanks and roar of jets grew louder by the day, and my sister wanted a harmonica!

Not long after Sheindy told me what she wanted, Mr. Lochte went to Celle on business. I asked if he could buy it for me. He agreed happily. The special day came. My sister Margarete turned fourteen. Congratulations! Mrs. Lochte made a birthday cake which she brought over to the Lauppers. We sat at the Laupper family's festively decorated table, Margarete/Sheindy received several gifts, and truly enjoyed the warmth and attention. What a treat, even if for a single day.

When I'd begun working at the Lochte farm, Mrs. Lochte had asked what salary I had in mind. Salary? Who even thought about such a thing? I hadn't come to work in this isolated village for a salary; I was just trying to survive the war. I'd been very surprised by the idea.

At Garssen we hadn't received payment, nor had the head of that village raised the subject. Unfamiliar with German money, I had no idea what kind of salary German workers received. Mrs.

Lochte thought I hadn't understood the question and repeated it. "How much do you want per month?"

My answer was that I'd be happy with whatever was acceptable. She looked at me, momentarily surprised, but then simply nodded. Quickly I raced over to Sheindy to tell her about this latest news, negotiations over a salary. It made us chuckle. "We'll come out of this war as wealthy people!" we laughed.

Apparently Mrs. Lochte had thought I was still too young to decide on such matters, and discussed it with Mrs. Laupper. Together they reached what they felt was an appropriate sum. And that put an end to the matter, which was never raised again. Not wanting to complicate our lives by showing our lack of knowledge about German money, we still preferred going to town on foot rather than by bus. Mostly, we didn't want them later talking about us for having taken advantage of them. Every time Mrs. Lochte offered to give me pocket money to spend on my trips to Celle, I refused, also taking sandwiches from home to save money. That was extraordinary in her view.

Towards the end of my first month of work, she came to me with cash in hand. "Here's what you earned this month," she said softly. I gazed at her, and then the money in her hand. "I'd prefer it if you would look after it for me because, if I take it, I'll spend it on unnecessary things." She obviously didn't expect that answer from me but agreed. I'm sure it seemed odd to her, but I often heard her praising me when she was quietly conversing with her husband. At the end of each month, she would say that she couldn't decide whether I was miserly or really wanted to put the money aside. Of course she couldn't have imagined any alternative scenario.

Once again, Sheindy and I headed for Celle, wanting to take the temperature of the city's mood. For hours we walked up and down the street but, unlike our previous visits, didn't see too many uniformed German soldiers. We concluded that it was a good sign. Of course we didn't go to the doctor, nor to eat lunch at the public soup kitchens. We decided not to visit Mrs. Redige, the Laupper family's aunt, either. We were on the lookout for one thing only: our own people. But after not catching sight of any Jewish refugees, we made our way back to Ohe, on foot as usual. An onlooker would have seen two German girls enjoying a walk through Celle's streets.

On our way back, we reminisced about our real families. We had no clue what might have happened to them, other than the fact that our parents, taken to Auschwitz with us, were probably murdered in the crematoria. We spoke a lot about our current situation, agreeing that signs of the war's imminent end were closer. We also agreed that we had to be doubly careful not to make any mistake so close to liberation.

Danger still clouded the air. That required acting with caution: not showing any happiness over the German army's approaching defeat nor making any slip of the tongue during these last weeks. We boosted each other's confidence and yet both of us were very fearful.

Post liberation plans: we had plenty of ideas, yet we had nothing tangible. Where would we go? How would we search for our parents? Would we find others from the family? Who could help us? Countless questions. Zero answers. We'd worry about it when the time came, solving each problem as we faced it.

Over the next few days the sirens, jets and tanks never stopped. We learned to live in the shadow of a war zone, not to think about the future, and to plan only for the shortest term: from morning to night, and night to morning. We were aware that anything could change at any moment.

Meanwhile, a new stream of German soldiers began showing up in the village as the retreat continued. Long convoys rolled past: tanks, lorries with soldiers returning from the front, the wounded. Everyone looked defeated. Officers weren't quite as tiptop as usual, nor did their boots shine like glass. I started fearing them less, but the sound of engines was enough to make the villagers tense.

The Germans had lost hope. They spoke openly about the war's end. "It's a matter of time," they'd say, "but which of the Allies would liberate the region?" The Germans seriously hoped it wouldn't be the Red Army.

On their way to work one day, cutting through the fields, the laborers found a parachute and brought it back with them. The paratroopers were here! Right here in our village! Maybe in the forest adjacent to Ohe, maybe even in the fields! Yes, now it really was a matter of time, perhaps just hours.

I was so emotional that I could hardly function. Mrs. Lochte thought it was because I was afraid of what might come and hugged me, promising to look after me and begging me to calm down. I ran to tell Sheindy the fantastic news. I kept fearing that I would appear pleased to my adoptive family or others in the village. What a dreadful mistake that would be. *We have no choice,* I kept thinking, *we must make sure not to show joy, not to show any change, in fact, and just hang on a bit longer until we're free. A little bit longer. Then living a lie will be over.*

As soon as Mrs. Lochte heard about the parachute, she went into the yard to take a look. I joined her, examining it inside and out. The fabric was red and white. I liked it. I asked if I could take some, and she looked at me, a bit stunned.

"What would you do with it?"

"Sew skirts for Margarete and me: a white one and a red one. Then maybe I'd sew one with both colors combined," I answered.

She gave me permission to take as much of the fabric as I wanted. She even laughed, saying that there was no end to the ways I could surprise her, but she did like the idea. She even offered me to use her sewing machine. That was an important element for me. Ever since stitching Sheindy's coat, I'd become the home seamstress, mending everyone's clothes or other items, as long as the repairs weren't complicated.

Taking apart one of Mrs. Lochte's skirts, I used the sections as a pattern. I sat for hours late into the night sewing skirts for us. Unbeknownst to her, I was focused on making these items because my clothes had been buried in crates for safekeeping. I wanted to get the sewing done quickly: my plan was to leave Ohe right after liberation.

Mrs. Lochte shook her head but smiled. What had gotten into me? But once she saw the finished item, she clapped her hands, pleased. I'd learned some sewing at school, until such time as Jews were no longer allowed to attend schools, following which I'd continued learning in a women's fashion workshop run by the Weingarten sisters. In retrospect, this lessons turned out to be very valuable.

JEWISH PRISONERS IN THE VILLAGE

Rumors were heard one day that prisoners in striped outfits with numbers emblazoned on their coats were wandering about Ohe. They reached the first homes on the village outskirts and began looting anything they could find, primarily food and clothes. Several prisoners also reached the Laupper's home. They shouted, ran amok, and tried their best to get inside. Mr. Laupper raced out with his rifle in hand and shot in the air. When he saw that didn't help, he shot one of them, killing him. The others, panicked, fled.

We learned that the Americans had liberated the concentration camps some days earlier and Jewish prisoners were out on the loose everywhere, especially in the villages, thinking they'd find food on the farms. They reached our village too. That's how we found out that the camps and their inmates had been freed. Hearing this, I was beside myself.

But Sheindy's and my situation was no less critical. German soldiers were no longer milling about in the village but neither were our liberators. It was a kind of an 'anyone's-guess' situation since there was no single leader in control and no one wanted to adopt responsibility. The German farmers withdrew into their homes, scared to go out to their fields.

On the other hand, the Ukrainians went crazy with joy, dancing, singing, getting drunk, celebrating the liberation that was yet to come. They pillaged the Lochte's basement, removing bottles of wine, fresh and preserved fruit and other food items stocked there, then went up to the first floor, broke into a room meant for smoking meat, and took whatever they could lay their hands on.

That night we no longer heard the tanks. A tense silence fell, broken only by an occasional shot. We had no idea what the next day might bring.

As morning broke, soldiers began to enter the village. A convey of lorries drove in. After soldiers entered our yard, we realized they were Americans! What a relief! But we were still too afraid to go out into the yard.

Curled up in the armchair, I was shivering. Was it the thrill of being liberated? Or was it trepidation about the future? Or both! The great day had arrived! I was free. I no longer need to fear, I can move about with my head held high and shout: "I'm Jewish!" Nevertheless, even though I desperately wanted to dash over to my sister, I didn't dare move from the room, especially since Mrs. Lochte had asked me to stay indoors. It was still unsafe outside, she warned.

The Ukrainian laborers had closed themselves up in their rooms, deeply disappointed. They'd been hoping for the Red Army and, instead, along came the Americans. They felt dejected – their plans had backfired.

There was knocking at the door and Mrs. Lochte, pale and shaking, opened it. Several soft-spoken officers entered and informed her that the American army had entered the village. They reassured her that they weren't going to harm them, they just requested that we carry on our lives as usual. The Americans took nothing, looted nothing, did not steal a thing. They were courteous and pleasant. In fact, the American conquest caused no shock waves at all.

I went upstairs to my room, shut the door, and thanked God

for bringing an end to the war and keeping my sister and me alive. We'd go home and begin new lives. I cried and laughed, and cried and laughed again. I was afraid to think about my family, relatives and friends. Had any made it through the war? Let's not think about that just now. I was so happy that tears streamed down my face.

The American officers in the Lochte home explained that because the house was the largest in the village, that's where they'd decided to set up their command center. They pointed to the ground floor rooms and set themselves up there. Günter and his soldier friend withdrew into Günter's room upstairs and didn't come out for several days.

Two days after the Americans entered, trucks rolled up to collect the Ukrainian workers. We had no idea who the drivers were or where the Ukrainians would be taken. They left without saying goodbye and we never saw or heard anything more about them.

Life did go back to normal. Sheindy and I were still viewed as German. We'd meet and speak at length about the current situation. Sheindy wanted us to leave the village right away, but I told her that there were still many matters to clarify before considering such a move.

Meanwhile we worked as always and tried to do everything to the best of our ability. A week after the Americans appeared we decided it was time to visit Celle again. This time we were not afraid to travel. On the contrary: we were thrilled. We had a goal: to attain the name of a central location where prisoners liberated from the camps could be found. We wanted to learn of our options for leaving Germany and, perhaps, heading home.

The idea seemed illogical: who would we possibly find at home? Who would receive us? We knew that our non-Jewish neighbors were living in our house and they probably wouldn't leave it simply because the war was over. We also discovered that our hometown had been taken over by the Red Army. It was almost certainly they would confiscate Jewish property and assets.

It was dawn and Sheindy and I were seated in the milk wagon on the way to Celle. We walked the now familiar city streets and couldn't believe our eyes: a throng of refugees meandering the streets, most still in the striped tops and pants, with striped hoods on their heads. Some wore civilian clothes; others were wrapped in blankets for lack of any warm clothing.

It very depressing sight: these refugees were painfully skinny, scared, and wandered aimlessly. Had any of our relatives or friends were among them, we wouldn't have been able to recognize them: they barely looked human.

How could so many refugees reach Celle so soon after liberation? We walked over to a group, wanting to ask a few questions, but were surprised to find they didn't want to talk to us. At last we come across fellow Jews, and they turn their backs on us? It took a while to understand that they thought we were German!

Our clothing and appearance most certainly could explain their conclusion. Sheindy and I both had blond hair and blue eyes. Our hair had now grown and was long enough to comb and style nicely. Outwardly we seemed like youngsters with no worries in the world. German teenagers.

Eventually we found a Hungarian woman amongst a group of refugees. We spoke to the group in Yiddish. It took a lot of effort to convince them that we were Jewish. Then the conversation changed completely, and we were the ones being asked questions. Where had we been during the war? How did we manage to survive for so long? They had a hard time believing us.

These refugees told us that a Jewish refugee absorption center had been established in Celle, where Jews liberated from the concentration camps were gathering. It was a large center, they explained, which already held thousands of Jews. There the Jewish refugees received a type of identity card that constituted certification that they were, indeed, refugees. With this important information now at our fingertips we said our goodbyes and headed for the center.

Knowing that there was now an authority to turn to, which would take care of us, made us very emotional. We would carry out all that was required to leave the village and move to the refugee camp. But when we reached the gate, an unpleasant surprise awaited us. Refugees crowding around the gate wouldn't let us in, again, thinking we were German! They shooed us away, shouting and throwing stones at us. None of our explanations helped. Two girls versus hundreds of fuming refugees: we had no choice but to distance ourselves from the gate, understanding the hatred they felt towards us. We couldn't blame them. But it did hurt that we weren't being acknowledged as Jewish.

I stood facing the road, watching them, unable to shift my gaze away, wondering if any of our family was among them. Relatives, perhaps? Friends? Neighbors? After all, the Germans took everyone. But how could we identify anyone? People's heads were wrapped in blankets or pieces of cloth pulled forward over their eyes and we could barely make out their faces.

The refugees made it clear that there was no way they were letting us into the center. They stood at the gate emphatically yelling, "Germans will not enter this center." Our hopes and dreams of getting a refugee identity card were shattered. We decided to go back to the village right away but, as we walked, I was already planning our next steps.

Although life carried on as normal and our adoptive families continuing to believe Sheindy and I were German, the liberation filled us with confidence. One day we decided to visit our cousin Mali at her workplace, the hospital in Celle. We weren't afraid of questions or interrogations anymore. We didn't feel threatened by the German government. We could carry our heads high.

Approaching the hospital's information counter, we told the

clerk that we wished to see Mali. She had left, he said, was now working as a translator in the American military camp and he wrote the address on a slip of paper. Grateful for the assistance, we left. Reaching our destination, we asked for her. She'd left Germany, we were told, and emigrated to America.

Mali was actually an American citizen who'd come to visit her mother in Europe. Unluckily for her, the war broke out and prevented her from traveling back. She was taken along with the other Jews to the ghetto, then to Auschwitz, and eventually ended up in Celle. When the Americans liberated the area, she lodged a visa request, immediately receiving the necessary papers from the US.

I'd been through so much with Mali. Older by several years, she lowered her age when questioned by the Germans and I raised mine so that we could stay together. We'd walked the march of death together, and fled the train together. Nor had we separated in the village of Garssen or Ohe, including our meetings with the Garssen village mayor.

Not wanting to draw attention to herself, Mali barely spoke despite being some years older than me. She was proficient in Yiddish but not in German, nor did she look like Sheindy and me. People in the village were always hesitant about believing she was our sister even though we presented her as such. They were pleased in Ohe when she left. We were sorry that she'd gone without saying goodbye, having made an effort to try and stay in touch, risking our lives to look for her in the Celle hospital. We had no idea where she'd gone, but she knew we were in Celle. We felt that she could have made an effort to let us know she was leaving.

Meeting Jewish refugees shook us to the core. We decided that we had to shed our outward appearance and somehow go back to being 'more Jewish.' It had been two weeks since the Americans had entered the village and we were still acting as

Germans. A tragi-comedy! Our immersion into our roles as German girls was so successful that our own people didn't believe we were Jewish!

What should we do?

We had to find a way to get into the refugee center and be acknowledged as Jews.

THE JEWISH OFFICER

The **American military** command was housed in the Lochte family's ground floor, but the Americans maintained good relations with the family members, ensuring that no problems would arise. One day an American officer entered the kitchen.

"I've got a pack of matzah from home!" he announced with great happiness.

My heart leapt. Seeing me, he thought I didn't know what matzah was and began explaining to me, the 'German' girl, that the Jewish festival of Pessach was approaching, when Jews did not eat bread, only matzah.

I was so dumbstruck I couldn't move or speak. A Jewish American soldier! Here! With me! What a coincidence.

Mrs. Lochte was also in the kitchen. I didn't want her to see any signs of excitement on my part, but my knees shook so much that I could barely stand up straight. Recovering from my shock and surprise, I realized that this officer could be my representative. He could help liberate Sheindy and me from our complex situation.

One day when I was alone in the kitchen, the Jewish officer came in to boil water for coffee. I mustered up the courage to take advantage of this opportunity and confide in him. I told him that I am Jewish, that I fled the concentration camp, that I have a sister also working in this village at the neighboring home, and that the villagers are convinced we're German refugees.

From the way he looked at me, he clearly didn't believe me and wanted to leave, speechless by what I'd told him.

I begged him to help me. I added that I know he's Jewish, that he received matzah from home for Pessach and that we, too, used to celebrate Pessach. Stunned, the soldier asked for more details about me, but I asked to set up a meeting with the colonel who visited the command center each week, and promised to share my whole story in his presence.

Wednesday came, and so did the colonel. Pale, shaking with emotion, I entered the colonel's office and sat at his desk, positioned in the room's center. To his right and left sat other officers, soldiers stood there too, because the rumor had spread about my forthcoming meeting. Everyone wanted to hear firsthand about this German-Jewish girl. My palms were sweating from excitement.

THE COLONEL, THE RABBI AND I

"**H**ow can I help you?" the colonel began.

I didn't want to stretch the story into too much detail, but I couldn't shorten it too much either. The room was silent, all eyes on me. The colonel spoke German, and I spoke a little English and fairly good German.

I described how Sheindy and I escaped from the train, how we waded through the stream during winter, how we reached the first village of Garssen and then continued on to Ohe. I told him that we took advantage of our appearance to impersonate Germans, how we obtained our German refugee certificates, and that Mrs. Lochte and her family had formally adopted me as their daughter. "But," I added, "we're Jewish." As proof, I showed the colonel the number tattooed on my forearm.

I spoke and spoke but he refused to believe me. Nor did the tattoo impress him. He said I was making it all up, that I must have carried out some serious crime, and now was looking for a way to flee Germany. He asked me to leave the office. I refused. I pleaded with him repeatedly to believe me, but nothing helped.

How would I prove my Jewishness?

And then an idea came to mind. If there are Jewish soldiers here, I reasoned with him, there must also be a rabbi. Please, let me speak to him!

The colonel sent for the rabbi, who appeared moments later.

I repeated the entire story to the rabbi and showed him the tattoo. But he, too, was non-sympathetic and incredulous. A

Jewish American rabbi had a hard time believing a seventeen year old, albeit with features of an Aryan, claiming to be Jewish! I didn't blame him: the story really was impossible to fathom. If this wasn't a life and death situation for me, I'd probably also have laughed at it. But there it was: having suffered so much because I was Jewish, I now had to prove that I was Jewish!

And then another idea popped up. I suggested to the rabbi that he ask me about Shabbat, Jewish festivals, and prayers, many of which I knew by heart. Liking that idea, he tested me on matters Jewish, asking about Hanukkah first. I described the festival, lighting of the eight-branched menorah, traditional foods and customs, and ended by singing the renowned Hanukkah song, *'Maoz Tzur.'*

Next he asked me about Pessach. Once again I provided details and sang *'Mah Nishtanah'* from the Pessach seder Haggadah. He asked about Rosh Hashanah and Yom Kippur, then I recited the blessings over bread, wine, fruit and so on. I did everything I could: talked, sang, recited, anything that would have him understand I'm Jewish. And, each time, I reminded him that my sister Sheindy was living with the family in the neighboring house.

This time, I did it! I passed the rabbi's test!

Clearly very moved, the rabbi informed the colonel that indeed I was Jewish. "These prayers which she recited can't be learned in a German family in a small village," he said. He realized what a terrible mistake it would have been to continue doubting me. At last he agreed, however, he added that he wanted to see my sister. A soldier was immediately sent to bring Margarete, to whom the rabbi addressed the same kinds of questions about prayers and customs.

At last! He agreed that we both were Jewish!

Upon hearing the rabbi's formal authorization confirming that we were Jewish, Sheindy and I breathed a great sigh of relief as the colonel, the rabbi and the soldiers congratulated us. They expressed their admiration at our resourcefulness, amazed at the actions we'd taken without any assistance; they praised us, voicing their wonder that we'd found a way to survive. "Good for you!" they smiled warmly.

"So, what was it you actually wanted to ask me?" the colonel brought the conversation back to its starting point.

I told him that the Jewish refugees believe we were German and won't let us into the refugee camp at Celle. I was seeking his assistance in going there, accompanied by his soldiers. The American Rabbi was still visibly very moved by our story, but promised that he would do everything to help. He told us how proud he was of us as Jewish girls who were able to survive and how, in fact, we were victorious over the Germans.

I hadn't said a word yet to Mr. and Mrs. Lochte, and continued working as usual. First, I wanted to be sure I had proper refugee cards in hand proving that I was Jewish, followed by authorization to enter the refugee camp. Only then would I tell the Lochtes the truth. I didn't want to hurt this good woman's feelings at all, however, as there was no alternative, at least let it be as minimal as possible.

On the appointed day, Sheindy and I arrived at the Celle Jewish refugee camp's gates accompanied by American soldiers. They tried getting us in but even they fell short. Refugees shouted, "Germans! Go away!" at us, pinched us, pulled our hair, and caused a huge ruckus around us. The noise brought even more refugees to where we stood, everyone threatening to tear us to shreds. The soldiers demanded that the guard lead us to the office. Linking arms, they encircled us, providing protection. It was the only way we could move forward. Slowly we made our way to the office amid shouts, curses and booing.

And once again, I told our story in the office. The manager wouldn't believe us, saying that this refugee camp only held Jews liberated from the concentration camps and, therefore, he couldn't acknowledge us as refugees. That's when the American soldiers intervened, saying that we held authorization from the rabbi that we are Jewish. That didn't help either. The office manager was obstinate, not even swayed by the tattoo on my arm.

I felt I was talking to a brick wall. I needed to find a solution, and fast, because the manager was losing patience. An idea! I asked him where the train with the open carriages which left Guben via Celle went, and had the prisoners in that train been made to walk the death march? Consulting with other clerks in the office, they concluded that the particular train had gone to Bergen-Belsen. So I asked to meet with other girls from there, because no doubt someone would be able to confirm my identity: after all, we'd been together, marched together, suffered together.

How tough it is to be Jewish! I was thinking, but to go back to being Jewish was proving tougher, by far.

An odd procession made its way from the offices to the women's residential building to look for girls who'd been with me in Greenberg and had arrived in Bergen-Belsen via Celle. In the lead was the refugee camp manager, followed by the vice-manager, and then came the two clerks and, following them were 'our' four American soldiers. We walked in pairs, the camp guards taking up the rear to keep us safe. And after all of this, a growing gaggle of curious refugee onlookers crowded about, having no idea at all what was going on.

Reaching the building, we entered a large hall where rows of beds lined every wall. Some young women lay on the beds; others sat on them. As soon as they saw us they began screaming, "Germans! Get out of here!" But the office manager asked me if I recognized anyone. I gazed at them: wrapped in blankets, it was hard to see their faces. How could I possibly identify anyone like that? Had my own sisters been here, I wouldn't have recognized them. I was incredibly tense to the point of dizziness, but decided that I would not leave until I'd found at least one person.

Cautiously I moved closer to the women, speaking in Hungarian, explaining who I was and why I was here. I reminded them of the night that the train pulled up at the Celle station and a number of women had fled the carriages after I had jumped out.

Suddenly a pale young woman wrapped in a blanket came towards me, only her eyes showing, and spoke quietly. "Hilda?" Initially I didn't recognize her, but hugged her and excitedly answered that it was me. It was as if, at that moment, the entire hall suddenly woke into consciousness. Leaving their beds, they came over. "Don't you recognize me? Rachel..." the one I'd hugged whispered.

Rachel had been in my row of five at the Greenberg camp. We'd always stood together. Another came over and said she remembered the night that we jumped from the train and how the Germans shot at us. She said that the German soldiers bragged how they had shot dead everyone who had fled, so she was sure I wasn't who I claimed to be!

Slowly others began recognizing me. What joy! The rumor spread fast. Young women came from all over the camp to see us, wanting to hear how we'd managed to survive, hiding with German families all these long months.

Back to the office we went, accompanied by a large entourage! Sheindy and I were given our refugee certificates at last. We were properly Jewish again! This card allowed us entry to the camp and provided us with the same rights as the other refugees.

We made our way back to the village. At the first opportunity, I thanked the American command center officer and the soldiers for their assistance, adding that I planned on sharing my secret with Mrs. Lochte the next morning, and requesting that they be at the ready to aid in any eventuality. Their presence infused me with confidence, because I had no idea how matters might develop once the family heard the truth. But one thing was clear: I'd tell them the whole truth.

Standing at the open window in my room, I breathed in the morning's fresh air. The snow had melted, spring was about, joy and hope filled my heart. I closed my eyes, imagining being home with my real family. I could see myself picking red roses from the yard, then playing tag with my friends among the trees. I didn't want to open my eyes: my imagination, my dreams, and reality intermingled.

Could I hear my name being called? Or was that part of the dream? Was I hallucinating? My sister stood in the yard below the window, calling my name. Had I not yet woken from my dream? I wasn't sure: which house was I actually in? Which yard?

But reality has its own agendas.

I opened my eyes.

THE TRUTH, THE WHOLE TRUTH

Usually I wore long sleeved dresses with narrowed cuffs to keep my tattoo hidden. But instead, dressing in the morning of the day I was planning to tell my adoptive family the truth, I snipped the seam open and rolled my sleeves up before starting my workday. I wanted the plaster on my arm to be visible. I was no longer afraid: there was no reason to be. But I was quite nervous and excited.

Obviously, Mrs. Lochte had acted in the way she had, looking after me, because she was convinced I was a true Aryan. I didn't want to hurt her feelings, because she really had been very good to me and we got on well. She gave me a home and a family, even adopting me formally, wanting only the best for me. But I'd lied to her without batting an eyelid, even if it was in order to survive.

I couldn't help wondering how her soldier son Günter would react. He'd probably have a fit. He played the role of the smart young man who understands everything, always having the final say.

Günter continuously tried to make me his friend, frequently suggesting that I join him on trips to the city for fun, for shopping, or to go riding together. Coming up with countless excuses, I always found a way to decline. He knew I was inventing them as a way of avoiding him. That angered him even more.

Mrs. Lochte was aware of the situation, but didn't want to

get involved. In this way he and I played cat-and-mouse, each of us waiting for the other to break.

By contrast, young Valter was a delight. He helped me with my jobs so that I could free up faster to play with him. I enjoyed every minute we spent together. There were no other children his age among the immediate neighbors, and our friendship took off from the start. I was happy to try all kinds of activities and games with him: horse riding, taking long walks. I agreed to all but one activity: swimming in the stream. Valter couldn't comprehend why I'd refuse. After turning him down several times, Mr. Lochte finally intervened and he stopped asking.

Mrs. Lochte was pleased to see that Valter was receiving attention and occasionally released me from certain chores just so that Valter would have a buddy. How would he react when he heard my story? He was twelve and had grown up in a home lacking for nothing: would he accuse me of deceiving him? He'd be right, of course.

Mr. Lochte: what would he have to say? Quiet, calm, a man whose company was pleasant, who was pleased to be consulted, who loved helping others. I remember how he received me that first evening, coming towards me in a welcoming manner. "I hope you'll feel fine here." And indeed I had.

As for Günter's soldier friend who felt an affinity for me because we were from the same city, he was inherently withdrawn and his presence in the house was barely noticed. Nor was his absence, when he went away for a few days.

Now that the war was over, I felt more certain, freer. Logic was guiding me on how to conduct myself, even if it was the logic of an adolescent whose parental guidance had been cut short at a young age. I knew I had to turn a new leaf and start from scratch. I knew the path would be long, difficult and wearying.

Taking a deep breath, I went down to the kitchen, wishing

everyone a good morning. Something in my behavior must have been different: perhaps I was a little quieter than usual, because Mrs. Lochte asked if I felt alright. She turned towards me, suddenly noticing my sleeves. "Hilda? What happened? Are you hot today?"

When I didn't answer she studied me more closely, noticing the plaster on my arm.

"Did you hurt yourself?" she asked with concern.

"No, I didn't," I answered.

"Then why the plaster?"

Our gazes locked as I stood facing her. She wasn't used to such short, sharp answers from me. I peeled the plaster away, showing her the number.

"But what is that?" she asked.

"My number."

She shook her head. "What do you mean, your number? Who did this to you? And why?"

Unable to hold back any longer, I began bawling uncontrollably, blurting out my story. For six months I hadn't allowed myself to cry in front of her, but now that the cork had been unplugged, I couldn't hold back. I cried over my parents and family, over the death march, over the suffering I had endured and what I'd seen. I cried over my people burned at Auschwitz who would never return.

Mrs. Lochte stood there, helpless and unable to comprehend.

Eventually I managed to get my words together. "Mrs. Lochte, I'm not German. I'm Jewish."

She shook her head, not believing me. "Hilda, you're lying," she said.

I was so emotional that I could barely speak. "I'm not lying now. These numbers were tattooed on Jews in concentration camps."

Bit by bit, I explained that everything I'd told her so far had been a lie.

"If you really want to know about me, ask questions and I'll answer," I said.

So Mrs. Lochte asked, and I provided the details: about my home, my family, the Germans taking us forcibly on cattle cars to Auschwitz, separating children from parents, how the parents were sent to the crematorium because they were considered too old to be entitled to keep living, about how we were used as cheap labor for the German Reich.

I told her how I managed to save my little sister and get her out of Guben so that we could be together, how we escaped the train in Celle, and how we waded through the shoulder-high icy waters of the creek in winter. I talked and talked and told her everything, like water coming out of a fire hose. I couldn't stop.

Mrs. Lochte's face had lost its color. She appeared scared. She asked more questions, and I answered. Then she ran to the field to bring her husband. I remained seated where I was, unable to move, unable to do anything, just trying to stay calm.

Meanwhile an American officer came into the kitchen and asked if I'd told Mrs. Lochte, adding that they'd heard me crying and understood that I must have. The officer calmed me down, saying that I had nothing to fear. "Be brave!" he said. "We're right here in the office and will help in any way we can." Glancing through the window he noticed Mr. and Mrs. Lochte approaching. "Stay strong," he reassured before heading back to his office. The fact that someone was watching over me, concerned about me, warmed my heart and infused me with the strength I so badly needed.

Mr. and Mrs. Lochte entered the kitchen. On the way from the fields back to the house, Mrs. Lochte had updated her husband of the news. They were both extremely emotional. On the other hand, I was suddenly calmer.

Mr. Lochte didn't know how to begin the conversation. "I see you told my wife that you're Jewish. Is that true?" he eventually began.

"Yes," I answered.

He gazed at me before responding. "Had you told us when you arrived that you were Jewish, we'd still have received you warmly and loved you."

I swallowed. "Have you forgotten the two Jews who hid in the neighbor's barn? Do you remember what you thought of them, how you behaved towards them? I couldn't take any risks and tell you the truth. I thought that as a German I had a greater chance of surviving the war."

"You told my wife," he added, "that the Germans burned people! We're not barbarians," he said. "We don't kill children and the elderly!"

So I described the Auschwitz crematorium, how the SS tortured us, their cruelty, the starvation, the shootings. I told him about my time in Kraków-Płaszów, paving roads during the nights, in the rain, in the cold wind and how, when we requested a brief respite, the SS would set their dogs on us, with comments like, "what a feast for our beast!" I told him how SS offices enjoyed watching us tremble with fear and scream in pain.

Mr. Lochte asked to see the tattoo. Interested, he asked about why this had been done. So I told him about concentration camps and how Jews were not considered human, stripping even our names from us and calling us instead by a number. I told him how everything was taken from us: parents, family, identity, and the will to live. I described the shower block where men shaved our heads and bodies because, in their view, hair was of value. And I detailed how we were brought into the shower stalls via one entrance, exiting from the other in a thin dress and wooden Dutch clogs. but I managed to keep the shoes I'd worn from home on my Papa's good advice, and how my naked back was beaten with a whip for keeping them.

Wanting to emphasize these truths, I reminded Mrs. Lochte of the coat my sister wore, with its red stripe on the back. This stripe was a mark of belonging to a concentration camp which is why, I explained, I pulled apart the entire coat and stitched it back up using the reverse side of the fabric. I showed her my coat with its patch on the back, underneath which hid the square of striped cloth sewn on in the Greenberg camp before the death march.

Dr. Mengele was next. I told them of his cruelty, of the monstrous experiments he forced onto children as a means of discovering ways to enhance the German race. I described 'selection,' and how he let children die of hunger to see how long they could last without food or water. My sister, I said, had been in the part of the concentration camp from which Mengele chose his victims, but a miracle had saved her when she was sent, instead, to work in the Guben forced labor camp.

Mr. Lochte sat listening quietly and intently. Every so often he muttered something like "I had no idea" or "I'd never heard such things." Actually, I believed him. Standing there, I answered all their questions but never once felt guilty. At some level I felt myself superior to the Germans: I had actually not taken anything gratis from them, nor killed their families, or cooperated with such actions.

Eventually Mrs. Lochte directed a question at me. "What are your plans now? Where would you like to go?"

Acknowledging the American soldiers, I explained that they'd helped my sister and me enter the Celle Jewish refugee camp because people there hadn't believed I was Jewish. Mrs. Lochte smiled. "You really do look like a German lass," she said. I explained that I want to join the refugee center in Celle and be among my fellow Jews, and perhaps even discover information about my other family members.

"And, despite all this," Mrs. Lochte said, sadly, "I'd love it if you stayed with us. After all, I adopted you as my daughter!" Repeatedly she asked me to consider staying.

"I have no idea," I answered, "whether any of my family has survived, or perhaps are waiting for me somewhere, but I must go and find out. I must search for them. Perhaps they're searching for me?"

As we conversed, Günter came downstairs and joined us. A tense silence fell. Günter was a controlling kind of person who could sometimes have a harsh voice and anger in his eyes. When he understood the situation, his emotions took over.

"For six months she was here and not a word of truth the whole time! And Hilda's sister, Margerete!" he shouted. "We need to call the cops! The district commander!" (although he did said that in a mocking tone). Günter couldn't calm down. "She took advantage of you! And you mean to say you never realized that? Then you reward her and adopt her as your daughter!"

He came up close to me, his eyes burning. "Why did you do it?" he hissed.

"Because I wanted to live," I said, quietly and simply. Then it was his turn to interrogate me. So I told him about Auschwitz, and the concentration camp where Germans tortured, murdered, and burned people alive.

Günter screamed that I was spreading lies and he didn't believe a word of the horrors I was making up. Then he fell silent. *I've won*, I thought. That gave me satisfaction. Eventually I told Günter that the day would come when he'd hear about these horrors enacted by his fellow Germans because the world would not allow the most massive crime in human history to be forgotten.

"You'll hear about the SS officers' cruelty, their crimes at Auschwitz and other concentration camps, and then perhaps you'll understand me better."

Wanting to shift the focus to him, I addressed him with a question of my own. "Why did you run away from the glorious German army?" I knew this was a weak spot. Had a cat got Günter's tongue? Judging by the lengthy sulky silence, I couldn't help wondering.

"I was injured!" he blurted at last.

"But the injury was an excuse," I persisted, "and, in fact, you deserted the army, scared stiff of the day they'd come to arrest you." I knew my statement insulted the very foundation of his identity. "The German army has collapsed," I continued, "and it's Hitler who brought destruction upon you and your country. He will be remembered in history as an insane person for leading the Third Reich into doom."

And then I fell silent. I was really agitated by now and needed to compose myself.

Actually, I hadn't intended to say those things, but Günter was trying to provoke his parents against me. Mr. and Mrs. Lochte sat quietly throughout, looking at him, then at me, and back and forth. I pitied this elderly couple who had no idea what to say. Most of all, my heart went out to Mrs. Lochte, who was broken and miserable after I'd shared my secret. In her eyes, I'd been one of the family and she'd heaped her love, concern and attention on me. Mr. Lochte had been no less kindhearted and good to me.

The American soldiers proved themselves considerate and likeable. They wanted to hear my story again and again. They asked questions, turning the story upside down and inside out, still having trouble believing their ears. The skeptics among them said that my story couldn't be true. Another asked again where we came from and how we reached this isolated village. I told them about Auschwitz-Birkenau, about Kraków-Płaszów, and other camps I'd been in. He'd never heard the names of these places, nor could he understand why the Germans would want to kill multitudes of Jews, going as far as to exterminate in gas chambers.

A weight lifted from my heart when I'd finally told my adoptive parents the truth, the whole truth. I was beginning to feel increasingly like my old self. The heavy load I'd borne for the past half year dissipated to a degree, allowing me to stand tall. Just knowing that I'd be leaving and that someone would look out for me raised my spirits. I was proud to be Jewish, knowing that, despite everything we'd been through, I wasn't alone.

I was eager to get to Sheindy and tell her that I'd shared our secret, that we no longer needed to be afraid. I wanted to hug her close and shout to the world, "Look! We're free!" But Mrs. Lochte said that, before I go to Margerete, she wanted to speak to Mrs. Laupper and prepare her, and would call on me to join them a little later.

When Sheindy saw Mrs. Lochte running to the Laupper home, she instantly understood the reason. Now it was all out in the open! She stopped her work, went into her room and waited. Not long afterwards, Mrs. Laupper called her downstairs. "Margerete, can you come down here please?"

Mrs. Laupper was in a state of shock from the startling news. Before my sister had time to come downstairs, Mrs. Laupper addressed her. "Is it true that you're Jewish? That you fled a concentration camp?"

"Yes," Sheindy answered.

And now Sheindy was asked all the questions: why, when, how, why had she lied. Sheindy explained that there were many reasons to believe that telling the truth would endanger us, as it had the two Jews who'd been found in the village.

By the time I reached the Laupper home, I found Sheindy crying. From fear? From joy? Perhaps a bit of both. It was clear that telling the truth had released the tension she'd been living under all this time. She was only fourteen, still a child and, if I'd cried, she was certainly entitled to cry too.

We went into the yard where I tried to calm her, hugging her tight. "We're free," I whispered in her ear, "so lift your head up and smile! We've made it safely through six months in German families, and it's already three weeks since the American army entered the village. But today we're finally liberated. Tomorrow we leave the village and start a new chapter of our lives."

One more hug and many kisses on my sister's cheeks, and

then I went back to the Lochte home. Valter came up to my room. He'd heard the story too, but couldn't quite put the pieces of the puzzle together. The one thing he did understand was that I'd lied. Now he was afraid to approach me but, at the same time, wanted to see me, probably curious to see whether being Jewish had changed me in some way or whether I was still the Hilda he knew.

Valter was as angry as a twelve year old boy who feels deceived can be. Nothing helped. He didn't want to hear any explanations. He simply repeated one statement several times. "You lied. You lied to us. You lied to me and I loved you." And then he ran away from my room.

LEAVING OHE

Mrs. **Lochte asked me** to fulfill one request before I left for Celle and the refugee center: to speak to the Americans who had taken over her home, using it as their command center, and tell them how well I'd been treated. She also asked me to write some kind of document certifying that I'd been with them for six months and was treated as well as the rest of the family. I was happy to oblige.

Mrs. Lochte explained how important it was for her that the soldiers wouldn't think ill of her, and that I was leaving of my own free will. I did as she requested even though the refugee center's office already knew of the high regard and esteem I held for the Lochtes and the Lauppers. I made my farewells from the colonel, thanking him for his help, and thanked the soldiers for being my escort into the Celle refugee center. I also wished the rabbi well and thanked him for helping me return to being Jewish. "If I hadn't heard this story with my own two ears," he said once again, "I wouldn't have believed it possible."

The next day Mrs. Lochte handed me an envelope filled with banknotes: six months of pay! "The money is yours, you've earned it, and it will be useful in the city," she smiled warmly. She also prepared me a food pack: bread, cheese, a bottle of milk, salami and cakes, "to be sure you have some food until you get organized in the city," she smiled again. What a moving gesture! We embraced and cried.

Standing in the yard waiting for Sheindy to join me, I was

surrounded by good people: Mr. and Mrs. Lochte, even Valter, and only Günter stood behind the house peering at me from a distance. He knew I could see him but I guess he was more comfortable not out in the open. Sheindy also arrived with a pack of food from Mrs. Laupper and an envelope with the wages she'd earned.

We learned that the two women had decided on this together. Mrs. Lochte asked me to visit her, saying my room "would always be ready, as would the little music box," she added, smiling warmly. She promised to send me food packages at the camp once a week with the milk wagon, and she kept her word. Every week the milk wagon's driver would send warm regards from the family. Mrs. Lochte was very upset that I'd left and was having trouble getting used to it, "because it happened so suddenly!" she wrote to me on one of her notes.

The Lochte family's farm was one of the larger in the region, employing some thirty to forty people who also lived on the farm. Now it was abandoned. The fields weren't ploughed, the furrows not sown with seeds, because no one was there to do the work. No workers had come to replace the Ukrainians who'd been shipped out. I was sorry that things were in such a state. When Sheindy and I were already seated on the wagon taking us to the refugee center in Celle, Valter came up to me and hugged me. "Please come and visit us. I love you, Hilda!" he whispered in my ear.

The wagoner tut-tutted the horse, cracked the whip, and off we went. We waved for a long time, until we couldn't see any of the family anymore.

A new chapter of our lives was commencing: we were heading for Celle. I breathed in the crisp spring air. As we approached Garssen, a spark of mischief flashed inside me. I would very much have liked to visit the Burgermeister and thank him too for his help on that fateful night, half frozen to death, hungry and shivering. But the wagoner, who knew nothing of our story, simply cracked the whip. We passed Garssen and the forest we'd hid in on the night we fled, the trees no longer snowy but lavish in new green leaves.

That night in the forest, we had no idea what to expect, what awaited us. We did all we could to survive, and yes, we'd done it! Was it just gutsiness? Was it destiny? Ensuring that at least some of our family would carry the family lineage to future generations?

THE CELLE TRANSIT CAMP

We settled in at the Celle refugee center and began planning and plotting our next steps. We needed to decide which direction we'd choose: America or Canada? Or should we perhaps return to Hungary? We free choice: all we needed to do was register our decision with the office. But we didn't yet know who, if anyone, of our family had survived. Was anyone left in Hungary? In Bratislava? We had many relatives in America, but I could only remember the address of our Aunt Ida. I decided to write to her immediately, explaining our deliberations and asking her advice.

Her answer came quickly. If we wished to come to America, she'd receive us both with love but, since the liberation was still fresh, perhaps we should try to find out if anyone else had survived. Knowing now that we had at least one address to turn to reassured us. I knew our aunt was right, and that we should first look for family who may have returned from the camps.

Time passed and Sheindy and I were still uncertain about our next moves. But everyone in the refugee center was dealing with the exact same issue. Day by day, my wish to see our family home grew stronger.

Every so often Sheindy went to visit our adoptive German families. On each visit she was warmly received, was asked about our plans, where we were headed, when. They were truly concerned for us.

I decided never to visit my adoptive family again, primarily because of Günter. For me, that was the best decision, but they always sent packages either with Sheindy or with the milk wagon.

Many, many more days of contemplation and consideration later, Sheindy and I decided to go home, to Hungary/Czechoslovakia but, because the war had so recently come to an end, there was a shortage of passenger trains and fuel. Thousands of refugees wanting to go home filled the Celle center. We had no choice but wait our turn, especially since we'd heard of trains getting stuck without fuel, or refugee-filled trains that remained parked in the station until an engine could be found to hitch up to the carriages. Those rumors discouraged us from making any moves too quickly.

Then came the day when we were informed our turn to travel to Czechoslovakia had arrived. Sheindy went to the village and informed both families that we were leaving Germany within the next several days. She embraced them warmly on both of our behalves before making her final farewells.

Refugee center staff provided us with some food for the journey but, from that point on, they told us, we'd have to look out for ourselves. We were brought to the station in freight lorries. And once again, the train was a long column of cattle cars, but at least this time we'd be traveling in the opposite direction.

We had some German money and were sure we could buy food along the way. When the train stopped in one of the villages, we went to a home to buy food. The farmers didn't want money: they wanted my sister's coat, the very same that I'd unraveled and restitched so that the red stripe no longer blared its presence. For one coat we received half a round loaf of bread and several potatoes.

The closer we came to home, the more our memories of our lives and family came into being. They were like a bittersweet dream. I didn't dare think about the reality. That would have driven me completely crazy.

The refugee train stopped at every station. Rumors had spread fast: Jews from the area would come to the station in hopes of finding family, relatives or friends. Fathers came looking for children. Women came looking for husbands. People shouted given and family names, running up and down alongside the carriages. The answers were usually either, "we hadn't heard any news of that name," or, "we don't know who they are." On rare occasions joyful encounters did take place. Mostly, there was disappointment. Refugees inside the carriages were also calling out names. The noise was deafening; the same scenario recurred at every station.

But the refugees weren't giving up. Again and again they asked about family members. Millions of family members hadn't returned from the concentration camps or forced labor camps, but the refugees inside the carriages and people standing on the platforms wanted to know, right now! Pushing through to the carriage door when we entered a station, I also called out names of my siblings: perhaps someone had met one of them, or heard the name at roll call. What had happened to my other two sisters, one of whom was married with a son? What had become of my brother living in Bratislava?

One day I stood on a station platform calling out my family's names. Someone came over, saying he'd known my brother-in-law, Zoli Adler. He told me that Zoli had returned from the camps and was now working in the UN offices in Bratislava, where everyone returning from the concentration camps was being registered.

Unbelievable! I'd found one person from our large family. Could there be others? Sheindy and I became emotional at this news: a light at the end of the tunnel, a filament of hope, someone to consult with... How amazing!

But what should we do now? Clearly we should detour and look for Zoli, but we were still on this crawling refugee train.

We thought up one plan after another but none seemed practical. In the end, after discussing the matter for hours, we decided to split up. I'd leave the refugee train and continue on a civilian train to Bratislava. If I found Zoli, I'd return with him to fetch Sheindy. If I didn't, I'd return to the refugee train to continue the journey. There wasn't a whole lot of logic to this plan, nor did we know the refugee train's final destination, but had any of the major decisions we'd taken until now been logical?

And so I left Sheindy in a corner of the carriage. It was hard to separate, but our hope was to meet again soon. I bought a ticket for Bratislava. I did remember Zoli's pre-war address, but was no longer sure he lived there. It'd be more likely that he lived elsewhere now.

Exhausted, nervous and stunned when I arrived in Bratislava, I hopped on a bus, showing the driver the address. He let me off near the Danube River and searched for 30 Hviezdoslavovo Námestie Street.

It took some time but I did find the house: a large home subdivided into two sections, with a shared entrance gate. Each section was further divided into small apartments.

Walking into the area left of the gate, I saw the tenants' names on letterboxes on the wall. Zoli's was in the last row. I couldn't believe it! Could the name have simply remained from before the war? I stood frozen on my spot, my heart pounding.

Facing the gate was a lone home which I presumed belonged to the concierge. The door was ajar. In the entrance stood a village woman selling her produce: eggs and milk. I went over and asked if by chance she knew someone in the building named Zoli Adler. She glanced at me, then poked her head into the house. "Zoli! Someone's asking for you!"

I began to tremble. The blood drained from my face. Going

inside, there he was: my brother-in-law, Zoli. I was so thrilled that I leapt at him, hugged and kissed him, and burst into tears. I couldn't hold back anymore. I cried and cried, but Zoli didn't react. He simply stood there like a pillar of stone, immobile, his hands by his sides. He didn't move to embrace me, he didn't smile, didn't react. His face held no emotion at all.

He was completely shocked. When Zoli married my sister, I'd been a little girl of five or six. I'd never really related to him as a brother-in-law because, for me at that age, he was like a much older brother bringing us, the little kids, gifts and sweets. We loved him very much and he got on well with my parents. I had only the best of memories of him. Everyone said that my sister Roza Rachel and I were almost carbon copies of each other. I'd once been shown a photograph of my sister when she was about twelve. The photo was compared to one of mine, and it really was hard to differentiate between us.

My brother-in-law hadn't seen me since before the war; meanwhile, I'd grown taller and looked very different. While living with the Lochte family I'd regained my strength, put on weight, become healthier, and looked nothing like someone freshly released from a concentration camp. I could feel Zoli trying to absorb what was happening. Taking a step or two back, I spoke quietly. "Zoli, remember me? You don't seem to recognize me. I'm Hilda, your wife's little sister."

Studying me, it was as if he had suddenly woken up from a trance. He smiled. I knew that smile. *Here, that's our Zoli*, I thought. When the excitement had died down a little, he wanted to know all the details. "How did you find me? How did you get here? How did you know I was back from the camps and in Bratislava?"

I told him about calling out names of family members at each station we passed through, including his name and how, at one of the stations, someone had approached and given me the information, mentioning that he worked for the UN. Sheindy was still on that train, I told him as I explained our plan. He listened, fascinated, not believing his ears.

"But why did you leave her on the train? Why didn't you bring her with you? And where's the train now?"

"I don't know," I said, because I didn't have answers about the train, "but right now the train's on its way somewhere."

He called over one of the clerks from his office, gave him a car, and ordered him to search for the train and my sister. "Don't dare come back without her!" he warned.

I wanted to travel with the clerk but Zoli explained that, since he had no idea how long the trip would take, it would be easier for the clerk to go alone and not have to look after me as well.

"So where's this train?" the clerk asked.

"No idea," Zoli answered. "Follow the tracks and let's hope you're lucky and find it."

The clerk drove off. My conscience was prickling. Why had I left her alone? Why hadn't I brought her with me? How would she get on without me? What a rash decision I made! Now I couldn't do a thing but wait. I was very worried and kept running to the office to ask if there was any news. Forty-eight hours later, the clerk returned – with Sheindy! I was so relieved, so happy for us to be together again.

"And that's what I did, follow the tracks, asking repeatedly about a train carrying refugees but getting no answers until, at a certain stop, the station master explained that the train was stuck somewhere along the way, that they were waiting for a supply of fuel to get it moving again, and that it could take days."

The clerk continued hunting until he found the train parked in the middle of an open field. Going from one carriage to the next, he called for Sheindy. He was amazed when so many refugees came to him with questions or requests, all wanting advice or guidance. People had been liberated from concentration camps but had found themselves in a now unfamiliar world.

They were worried in general, and had no idea how to go about beginning their lives once again.

Zoli's clerk said that he went calling Sheindy's name, looking for blond hair and blue eyes.

Suddenly from the corner of a carriage he heard a weak voice responding, "I'm Sheindy/Margerete. Are you looking for me?" The clerk breathed a sigh of relief. "Yes, I certainly am!"

He went on to explain who he was and why he'd been sent, asking her to come with him in the car to Bratislava and back to Hilda and Zoli.

But that turned out to be easier said than done. Sheindy wasn't willing to move from where she was seated. Saying that she had no idea who he was, she wasn't about to go with him to who-knows-where, and that she was waiting for her sister Hilda to come back.

He used all his persuasive energies to convince Sheindy to come back with him. He explained that Zoli explicitly said not to come back without her. Eventually he succeeded in coming across as credible. And here they were, at last.

Sheindy and I took a little time to recover from our reunion and then went out for a walk, enjoying the sun's warmth. Pleasant hours were spent on the Danube's banks, the river not far from Zoli's place. Time passed, expectantly awaiting word from others in the family. We had no information about our sisters who, when the war broke out, were in Budapest. Had they been deported to Germany? Had they been lucky and survived somehow?

Our Papa, an injured veteran of the First World War, as it was now known, had enjoyed several rights such as exemption from wearing the yellow star. He'd received a special certificate listing his impairments and had sent similar certificates to my two sisters in Budapest. I remained hopeful that perhaps those certificates had helped them stay in Budapest and not be deported to Germany.

THE FIRST MOVE AFTER THE WAR

Bratislava **gave prominence** to the sense of freedom. For the first time, I wanted to laugh, to sing, to run through the streets. I wanted to prove to myself again and again that I really was liberated at last, master of my destiny, free to make plans for the future.

It was summer now, and the days were sun-drenched and optimistic. Walking along the Danube was so refreshing. Wandering through the city was so inspiring. Watching people in the streets was so heartwarming. Gazing into shop windows was so exciting. I was sure new blood was coursing through my veins. The world looked so busily beautiful.

Huge lettering on the poster pasted to the cinema's wall announced that day's movie, "Humoreska," featuring Dvorak's piano pieces titled "Humoresques" and starring Czech actress Hana Vítová! A strong urge swept through me to see it. I bought a ticket and went inside.

The theater was spacious and almost filled to capacity. *People seeking entertainment after the war,* I thought, *looking for a reprieve from what they experienced in the camps. Why not buy an hour's worth of illusion before leaving the theater to continue the fight for survival?*

It was the first movie I'd seen since the war was over. Every minute was a delight. Dvorak's 'Humoresque' plays in my mind to this day! I remembered movies I'd seen with friends as a child, movies with cute little Shirley Temple; movies with Charlie Chaplin; movies with Johnny Weissmuller as Tarzan.

One day Zoli took me to a shoe store and bought me a pair of patent leather shoes which reminded me of the ones I'd left behind in the train to Auschwitz. I stuffed my ankle boots into the box which the new shoes had come in. They were the only item I had left from home. How could I possibly throw them away? Only when I left Bratislava did I leave that box behind, with Zoli.

Life began to take on a kind of routine but, throughout that period, I was bothered by images of the moment I'd encountered my brother-in-law. I remembered how he'd just stood when I came in, as though fossilized when seeing me for the first time. What was going through his mind? Knowing that something had happened to him in those moments, I was curious to discover what.

Eventually I asked him outright. He gazed at me for some long minutes before saying that, when I entered like a tornado, he was completely taken by surprise. Everything happened so fast that he hadn't even got a good look at me. The only thing he registered was that someone who looked like his wife had walked in.

In that flash of a moment, he could only wonder: if his wife had just walked in, where was his son? Miki would have been eight. Had his wife willingly separated from their child? Had she been forcibly split from him? So many thoughts spun about, confusing him.

Sensing this, I'd taken a few steps back. Then he was able to see me more clearly and recognize me. And that's when his familiar smile spread across his face. He held his arms out and hugged me, and that's when I cried and cried into his shoulder: crying for my parents who I'd never see again, crying for the family who wouldn't return from the extermination camps, crying for the terrible suffering I experienced.

SHEINDY VISITS OUR AUNT

At some point in time, information reached us that our aunt, who lived in the spa resort Trenčianske Teplice in Czechoslovakia, had hidden successfully during the war in her hometown, never taken to the concentration camps.

Before the war, I'd met this aunt when she would often visited us with her daughter. What if I sent her a letter to say we'd survived the concentration camps, and we're now with Zoli in Bratislava? Her response wasn't long in coming: she was so happy to hear we were back and invited Sheindy to come. She would take responsibility for Sheindy's continued education, living expenses, and all her needs. What a generous offer! I was pleased to know that someone from the family was taking an interest in us.

Lengthy deliberations later, we decided that Sheindy should indeed go. We packed her suitcase and took her to the station. It was beyond difficult to say goodbye, but I promised Sheindy that I'd visit soon. One of Zoli's close friends, a Russian Jewish officer, agreed to accompany her. In those days train travel was truly dangerous, all the more so for children, and especially young girls.

Sheindy was looked after by the officer an handed over safe and sound to our aunt, but my sister's dreams of a warm loving family evaporated. It wasn't long before it became clear that our aunt's promises were just empty words. As soon as Sheindy arrived, our aunt took her to the Population Registrar and appointed herself as Sheindy's legal guardian, then took her refugee card from her and, with it, all the rights to which Sheindy was entitled, including a large apartment and a shop. The aunt never gave Sheindy a moment of attention or love, and no pampering of the kind Sheindy so desperately needed after getting through the war.

Sheindy wanted to register for school and return to her studies. After all, that had been the primary purpose of her trip. But the aunt repeatedly prevented that. Some weeks had passed with Sheindy not rejoining any study program. She had no one with whom to consult, no one from whom to seek advice, but her logic told her that she must not, under any circumstances, continue to stay with her aunt.

When the aunt was out one day, Sheindy tossed her clothes into her suitcase, gathered up photos of our family that we'd sent the aunt when life was still good before the war and, without saying a word to anyone, went to the train station, bought a ticket, and returned unaccompanied to Bratislava. Not long afterwards our aunt telegrammed us: Sheindy had disappeared. The aunt had called the police to look for her. We messaged back:

No need to look for her stop she is in bratislava stop she will not return to trenčianske teplice stop.

THREE SISTERS

Sheindy and I went for a walk in Bratislava and – who do we see coming towards us, grinning from ear to ear – if not Zoli! And a girl! Once they were close enough, I couldn't believe my eyes. Our sister Hannah! There we stood in the middle of the street, three very emotional sisters, hugging, kissing, crying, laughing. Tears rolling down our cheeks. Tears of joy and pain, of loss and good fortune. How happy we were. We sat up until late at night, each of us detailing our survival stories.

Hannah told us how she and our other sister, Goldie, also known as Zahava, managed through acquaintances to be slotted for work in the Jewish hospital as nursing assistants. They not only worked there, but lived inside the building, doing their utmost to never go outdoors which could get them caught.

The Swedish Consulate issued a certain number of protection certificates, the Schutz-Pass, which helped Jews avoid deportation to concentration camps although, towards the end of the war, these passes no longer protected their Jewish bearers.

Using skilled contacts, the Budapest Jewish Committee forged large quantities of these passes, handing them out to refugees coming into Budapest. This is how my sisters ended up with forged Schutz-Passes which helped keep them in Budapest throughout the war. A large number of Jews were saved by these certificates.

Hannah's stories also included funny incidents. One day, for example, the hospital guard nervously raced up to the Chief

Physician, telling him that German soldiers would be coming to run checks in the departments. It would be better for the SS not to see the forged documents. Without giving it a second thought, Hannah lifted up an old man's blanket and lay down next to him, covering herself fully, over her head, lying there until the Germans left. The old fellow, shocked, almost had a heart attack.

After the war, my two sisters joined the Budapest branch of the 'Hashomer Hatzair' Zionist secular youth movement. Shortly afterwards they traveled to Bucharest, intending to emigrate to Israel. But there in Bucharest my sisters heard from other refugees who'd passed through the UN offices in Bratislava that we'd returned from the camps and were staying with Zoli. Initially they found this impossible to believe: how could two little girls like us survive? Hannah decided to see for herself.

This was our first encounter after the war. Once we'd caught our breaths, the three of us and Zoli raised ideas about planning our future. We were psychologically exhausted and wanted nothing but quiet, a warm home, and security. We had to come up with a plan for our post-war lives without parents or a home.

Zoli suggested that I stay in Bratislava to continue my studies. Hannah didn't agree. She didn't want to leave me ever again. "After all," she justified herself, "we've only just gotten together at last!" That decided the matter: the three of us would travel to Budapest.

Zoli was wonderful, making sure we had everything we needed, giving us support. But the end of our moving from place to place, from country to country, had not yet arrived: we needed to move on. Would there ever come a day when we'd be able to feel secure in our homes? Where would our homes be? And when?

So much was still unknown.

Leaving Zoli, we were overcome with emotion, but on we went to Budapest.

BUDAPEST

On a bright sunny day we arrived at the Hashomer Hatzair kibbutz in Budapest known as the 'First of May Kibbutz.' *At last*, I thought, *an end to moving around.* But no. I was the youngest among the girls there and they didn't want to accept me, claiming that my place was with the Youth Aliyah movement, or Aliyat Hano'ar as it was commonly called: youth emigrating to the Land of Israel. I was so discouraged, I wanted to throw in the towel.

Hannah vehemently opposed the decision and refused to let me go. A members' meeting was called to deliberate. Opinions were divided: one group was for, the other against. Lengthy, numerous discussions were held until the decision was reached. Fortunately the 'for' was the majority. I stayed in the group, immensely grateful.

Integrating into kibbutz life was fast, good, smooth. The group comprised young people of around the same age, all of whom had experienced the Holocaust, all of whom were seeking a home, love and a bit of attention. A group of lonely people whose souls had been harmed, who had no parents, no families, but we had a shared hope and desire: to find a better future.

Sheindy was accepted into an Aliyat Hano'ar program which included studies. This aspect was important to both Hannah and me, particularly the social element of being in a group of her peers. Another farewell, but this time one we agreed upon, in the hope that all four of us, the remnants of our family, would meet up again soon in the Land of Israel.

Several months after joining Aliyat Hano'ar in Budapest, Sheindy's group traveled to Vienna, then to Ansbach in Germany where they waited for their turn to emigrate. Meanwhile Sheindy fell ill. The doctor diagnosed damage to her lungs. She was sent to a tuberculosis sanatorium in the German Alps to recover.

Sheindy spent a full year at the sanatorium undergoing extensive treatments until she could rejoin her group, still waiting in Ansbach. Once their turn to emigrate came around, they traveled to Marseille, France. In the port city of Brest they were put on the immigrant ship 'Exodus,' later dubbed 'The Exodus from Europe.'

While we continued waiting in the kibbutz group in Budapest, Hannah decided to visit Sevluš to see our family home one last time. Would she meet family, friends or acquaintances who'd returned? Regrettably, she was deeply disappointed. Countless refugees wanted to visit their homes. These visits typically ended with the same outcome: they didn't find their families, their homes had been commandeered by the Ruthenians, the contents usually looted by neighbors. Hannah discovered that our home, too, had been taken over by Ruthenian neighbors.

Hannah stood in front of the house like a beggar, her heart filled with longing, peering over the fence because the neighbors wouldn't let her in. Yet Hannah was obstinate, persistent and sat down next to the gate, telling them she wouldn't move until they let her inside. Our former neighbors consulted with each other, eventually agreeing to open the gate. Her heart pounded as she stepped in.

Pushing the door open, she looked up. Her eyes began to water. There on the wall facing the front door hung a massive crucifix. Against that wall had been shelves holding Jewish prayerbooks, bibles, and other holy texts. Nothing was left of the items that had been ours. Hannah walked outside, wandering around the yard and garden. Our apple tree had been of a special kind that produced clusters of large fruit. All our neighbors used to come and look at them in wonder.

Hannah put her hand out to pick an apple. The new owner quickly stopped her, saying that the fruit was now hers and Hannah had no right to pick any. Nonetheless Hannah managed to leave the garden, apple in hand, tears rolling down her face. She also requested the family photos left behind, but was told they'd been thrown in the garbage two days earlier. She ran to the garbage heap and did manage to save several. Despite being torn and dirty, they were worth more to us than gold.

With her apple and our family photos, Hannah left.

ALIYAH TO ISRAEL

Jewish youth movements in Budapest began organizing frameworks for young Holocaust survivors. I also joined those planning to emigrate to the Land of Israel under the auspices of the secular Zionist movement, Hashomer Hatzair. For five months we were trained on how to run a kibbutz.

During this period, the group consolidated and readied for Aliyah. The word's meaning was explained to us: the word 'Aliyah,' meaning ascension, applied only to Jews emigrating to Israel. When the awaited day arrived, we loaded our rucksacks onto our backs yet again, and headed for the boat which would take us there.

Our journey to the 'Bracha Fuld,' a boat anchored in Italy, was replete with its own ups and downs. Post-war Europe was a dangerous place and, once again, we had to hide our identities and slip across borders until we reached Rome. For a year we were stuck there, although we lived active lives.

One night our leaders assembled us in the forest, announcing dramatically: "The time has come to break through the gates of our homeland!" Immediately afterwards, military trucks covered in canvas took us to a secret location in southern Italy. In the dark of night, in small rickety boats, we were brought to where our ship anchored. Climbing rope ladders, 806 Jewish refugees whose greatest desire was to reach safe haven at last, boarded.

A SHIP CALLED 'BRACHA FULD'

Before dawn on October 8, 1946, the little 'Bracha Fuld' of a mere 400 tons raised anchor, setting sail for Israel's shores. The boat's commander was Menahem Cohen, later a colonel in the Israel Defense Forces. With him was an Italian captain who agreed to join the arduous, dangerous journey. Their crew was a group of young Israeli men helping thousands of refugees in Europe.

Life on board was conducted with supreme discipline. We stood in lines for meals, for the bathroom, and even to stand on deck and get some fresh air. Everything was meticulously organized. We were allocated one liter of water per day and slept on sleeper mats that could only be reached by crawling to them. The Israeli lads chose a group from among us to help them maintain order and control.

The day after we embarked, the sea began to get stormy. The commander was forced to close all air apertures. It was an awful scene: people began to suffer from sea sickness and dizziness. Hardly anyone could eat the improvised meals cooked by the Israelis and their helpers.

Once we reached southwestern Greece, not far from the island of Spetses, we were sure we'd been saved from the sea that had tossed our little ship around, but it didn't quite turn out that way. The boat's engine, it appeared, had died. Our little tub was bobbing uncontrolled in the waves, drawn towards the tall cliffs, the danger of capsize hovering over our heads.

The captain ordered the team to raise sail, hoping that it would help us float better until the engine could be fixed. Our Italian sailors were suddenly consumed by fear and couldn't do it, but the commander, whose clear-headedness in the face of crisis was amazing, somehow infused them with confidence until they cooperated. The storm was whipping up, the waves washed over the boat, thunder and lightning constantly threatened us.

The commander sent a telegram to his superiors about our predicament and the imminent dangers while simultaneously continuing his efforts to stabilize the boat. The mechanics worked tirelessly on repairing the engine. We, the refugees, lay in the hold, not knowing anything about what was happening. We were tossed around. We suffered from nausea. We feared the lightning and thunder. Some began to curse Herzl for 'inventing' Zionism, never mind that it's a millennia-old Jewish concept. Others began shouting as they fell into a state of panic.

Hearing the refugees screaming, the commander went down to us and hushed the tumult. He explained that the engine would be fixed and calmed everyone's nerves. Some people cried. Others encouraged him. So we lay there, praying that matters would work out for the best. In the distance we could see the scary shores of Spetses. Our air apertures were still clamped shut. We placed wet towels on our faces to ease the unpleasantness.

At a distance of some five hundred meters from the cliff, a roar was heard. The engine was up and running! Music to our ears! A joint sigh of relief was breathed. Not long afterwards we saw the lights of Haifa, the city on Israel's northern shores. A fantasy, a legend coming true.

CYPRUS

Did we reach safe haven?
No.

Britain was the Mandatory entrusted with the administration of the Land of Israel at the time. They viewed us, exhausted refugees that we were, as a conquering army, and ordered us banished from the land. Four British battleships sailed out to surrender our little refugee boat. We were forcibly taken off board and transferred to an expulsion ship which set sail for Cyprus. There, in the middle of nowhere, as far as we were concerned, we found ourselves in a camp surrounded by guards!

We were divided into groups of eight and set up in tents, one bed to every two people. There were no bed linens. There were no clothes. But we quickly learned to utilize the cloth used as tents for a whole variety of other purposes, sewing ourselves everything we needed: pants, sheets, pillowcases. Water was brought in containers, food was canned goods. There were no books, of course, but with our shared memories we managed to set up a cultural program to which each person contributed their personal experiences.

For more than half a year we were in Cyprus until authorization was received for our Aliyah. When we at last reached the Atlit camp not far from Haifa, we found it to be another kind of closed camp. Two months later we were transferred to Kiryat Shmuel, a suburb of Haifa, where we were once again surrounded by barbed wire fences. It took a while but eventually we reached Kibbutz Ma'anit, and an end to our journeys. But by now it was the summer of 1948, and the War of Independence had begun. Unsurprisingly, our group was sent to frontline positions and night guard duties.

FIFTY YEARS LATER

Fifty years have passed since we were expelled from our homes. My children, having grown, expressed their interest at visiting my hometown but I kept postponing the journey year after year. I was afraid of going back to my city of birth, to the place from which my family had been banished, not knowing how I'd feel when seeing the familiar vistas, the street, the house I was raised in.

I was also hesitant about traveling there with my children, fearful that something might happen to them there.

My husband, Moshe, who had since passed away, promised to take me back, but while the Russians controlled the region no tourist visas were being issued. Once they did eventually allow tourists, Moshe was already too ill to travel.

My children, though, weren't giving up so easily. Repeatedly they asked when we'd visit Sevluš, now known as Vinegradeve. We need to close the circle, they told me. Yes, our father has passed away, and we want to fulfill his promise.

So one day I gave in, and we set a time that suited us all. A trip home, accompanied by my family! Simultaneously excited yet fearful: I had to know I'd come back to what was *now* my home, with them, safely.

We decided in advance that we'd document this trip, and each of us were given a task. Gadi and Valerie were in charge of filming. Tziki and Nurit would be the photographers. I took on the job of writing, documenting the experiences of these encounters, but found I couldn't do it. Some of the time I was assisted by a recording device but, eventually, I did log our experiences from memory once I was back home in Israel.

A visit of this nature requires excellent planning. Drawing on the experience of my sister, Yaffa, who had traveled back to Sevluš forty-seven years after our expulsion, we prepared ourselves. Yaffa's trip had been fraught with complexities, including discovering that the family home's iron gate had been covered with iron plating and locked tight, making it impossible to even peek into the yard.

An elderly woman who happened to pass by wanted to help Yaffa. The woman had actually known not only our parents, but us too, when we were kids. Nothing helped: that gate was jammed shut. "The woman living there now is refusing to open up and let you in," the passerby explained. Yaffa, as Sheindy had been called since coming to Israel, stood there outside in disbelief: how could this be happening? She had no choice but to take a photo in front of the house and leave, crying as she went.

After Yaffa's upsetting experience, we decided to contact Rabbi Oberlander, head of the Budapest Chabad House, asking him to contact the Farkas family, a Jewish family still living in Sevluš, to prearrange our visit to our family home.

On August 9, 1993, our little entourage set out. My son Gadi and his wife Valerie, my daughter Nurit, my son Tzvi, and me. In Budapest we were met by Rabbi Oberlander who advised us to stock up on food and water in Hungary because, in Ukraine, he explained, "you won't be able to find any food." At the time we had no idea how true that would be.

Hiring a car with an accompanying driver, we set out. We reached the border in the afternoon. Getting through border control procedures at Chop-Záhony took three hours. At last we were in Ukraine. The roads were dreadful, they carried very little traffic, the surrounding fields appeared neglected, the wheat and sunflowers visible from the car much lower in height than they should be, meager rather than lush.

Another four hours of driving brought us to Munkács (Mukačevo), where we'd booked hotel rooms for two nights. Munkács looked forlorn, desolate, as though time had stopped for fifty years. We managed to find the hotel with the courteous assistance of two Ukrainian soldiers who volunteered to accompany us there. When we pulled up in its yard behind the building, we were sure we'd arrived at a prison!

Gray, oppressive, plaster shedding from its walls, the structure was surrounded by filth and mess. Only when we reached the so-called lobby did we understand that booking in advance had been unnecessary. Despite having some two hundred rooms, only seven or eight were occupied, among them the four of ours!

Clearly this building had known better days. Now it begged thorough renovations, but Ukraine's economy at the time made it clear no fixes would be forthcoming in the near future.

We filled in the registration forms at the reception desk, were handed our keys, and then asked the reception clerk about the dining room: it was closed for tonight. What should we do? The city was dark, the streets empty of people; here and there a lone streetlamp flickered. Pointless to even think of a restaurant that might be open.

We congregated in Zvi's room, Gadi pulled out the food we'd purchased in Hungary, and set up a table, slicing the bread and inviting us to the 'buffet.' We laughed and chatted until our sides were splitting from this tragi-comic situation. Our driver suddenly discovered that under the bed was a wiretap! We had no idea if it was working, but our driver, suspicious, disconnected all wires leading to the device.

The reception clerk informed us that rubles were no longer acceptable in Ukraine. They had been replaced by notes about the size of a cigarette pack, known as vouchers. A laborer's average monthly salary was 200 vouchers, which equated to ten kilograms of meat or 877 liters of cream. Without vouchers nothing could be bought in the shops. A loaf of bread: 5 vouchers. Compared to the average salary, that was extremely expensive. There were no lines outside the shops anymore, because not everyone could even afford to buy bread.

Munkács's homes showed the ruination of time: peeling walls, gardens neglected for the most part, an odd flower popping up here and there. Vines still grew freely over fences. Trees still greened. Almost every home was fronted by a wooden bench, typical of villages in this region. Walking on the roadside were women bearing several kilograms of tomatoes or prunes, possibly from their own gardens, waiting for random buyers.

The next morning we were off to Sevluš. We left the hotel knowing with certainty that we wouldn't be returning. My heart began pounding, my knees wobbled. Alternating waves of heat and cold swept through my body, a sign of rising emotion.

At the entrance to the city of Sevluš, to the left, apartment blocks had been built: long rows, with balconies. I was happy to see flowers alongside clean pavements, and traffic, Russian of course, up and down the streets.

To the right stood the hospital which I remembered so well. Getting out of the car, I approached the building, my eyes filled with tears. This is where Papa had been hospitalized several times as a result of his WWI injury. We, the children, would bring him kosher meals, cooked by Mameh. Images of the past raced through my mind.

My first thought was that I had to get control of myself, of my memories and sorrow. Then I thought: but why? Why shouldn't I cry out loud? Why shouldn't I scream? Why shouldn't I release everything that I've held inside for the past fifty years? If there were ever a time and place to do that, it would be now! But a solid lump caught in my throat: I sobbed quietly. Sensing my distress, my children stood close, supporting me. What a comfort.

We drove on. Fifty years later, the city seemed very different to what I remembered, but much cleaner than Munkács. We went to meet Rubi, the Farkas family's son, who would be accompanying us in Sevluš. From that point, our visit in the city became far simpler.

Our first stop was the city center where my parents' shop had stood. Long ago it had been destroyed for the sake of road expansion work, but I remembered the location and the general region. I showed my children the Catholic church adjacent to which had been the kosher butcher, next to that the greengrocer, and then my uncle Shimon's shoe repair store. I remembered how the shoes and boots hung in rows on planks nailed to the ceiling. Having described these images to my children, I then translated into Hungarian so that Ruby would also feel included.

Suddenly two women walking down the street stopped to listen. They were Jewish and confirmed my description. "Yes, you remembered that correctly," they agreed. I continued with my memories from this place: the street corner where the watchmaker Klein and his family lived: their children now live in Netanya. The family's home had been razed, replaced by a multistorey apartment block.

Remembering every detail, I pointed to a house where the Weiss family had lived. I'd gone to school with their daughter, who now lives in Israel. But these memories weren't easy to cope with, and overexcitement caused my skin to break out in a rash. I loved my birth city, the Tisza River a mere half hour's walk from our home, the Carpathian Mountains visible on the horizon. I loved the grape harvest season, which I'd joined every year as soon as I was old enough because all hands were needed.

The two Jewish women continued to stand with us. One had a daughter in Israel and wanted me to take a letter for her. But time was running out and we needed to return that same day to Hungary, rather than stay in the Munkács hotel. We said our goodbyes to the two women and went on our way. The small bit of Russian I'd learned at school actually did help on this trip because the city and street names were written in Cyrillic lettering, which meant I could read them easily.

We reached the corner of our 'Russian' street and parked. From there I wanted to walk the four or five houses, feeling the ground beneath my feet. My children walked with me. The driver slowly drove alongside.

It was all so odd, so strange. A mix of memories and dreams. House after house, I noticed that the numbers had been changed. I walked on, slowly, carefully, one step, another. Was I afraid of the memories, or of facing the current reality? Probably both.

Our home, which had been number 29, was now number 7. Yes, there was our house! High up on the wall was the wheel we'd used to raise various objects up into the attic! Stable and steadfast, the home seemed to be waiting for its true owners to return. It had withstood the test of time; no more than a coat of paint was needed to spruce it up to its pre-war state.

There was the tiled roof, the fireplace chimney reaching skywards. It's where we dried black plums, replacing the pits with nuts. Then we'd place the plums in bags and hang them on a rod in the chimney to dry them out. In winter, when other trees in the garden were snowed over and our windows were covered in frost, those smoked prunes were such a delight.

Because the house numbers had been changed, a small mishap occurred. We'd asked Rubi to help arrange a visit with the family in our house, but Rubi had made arrangements with the people in number 29, not realizing the numbers had changed. We were afraid that the people in number 7 would treat us as they'd treated my sister Yaffa.

Despite the numbering. I had no doubt which house was ours. This is where I was born and grew up. It's where the scent of bread being baked in the outdoor oven filled the yard, where confitures were boiled in large copper vats, where the walnut tree, the plums and other fruit grew in the garden. How well I also remembered the mix of languages spoken at home, in the street, in the market and at school. Belonging: that's what I felt the instant I laid eyes on our home.

The woman living in our house saw people gathered in front of 'her' home. Opening the window hesitantly, she asked if we were looking for something. Rubi explained the purpose of our visit. Immediately she agreed to open the gate. Stepping forward firmly but trembling inside, I entered, stopping for a moment at the entrance as I had so many years ago, returning from school, Mameh appearing at the door to welcome me home.

Now someone else stood there, a smiling Hungarian woman inviting me to enter my own home! The act of standing at the entrance had been in my thoughts night and day since we decided to make the trip.

***

For years I hadn't dreamt of my parents. Now, as the trip neared, I dreamt that I was running through the gate to find Tateh seated in the yard on a large stone. "I was waiting for you," he said. I woke in a sweat and decided to cancel the trip. Later I reneged. This occurred on multiple occasions. Yes, no. Yes, no. Yes. Here I was at last in the yard's center looking for the large stone of my dream, but all I saw in its stead was a pile of junk metal.

***

A fifty-year-old dream was coming true but all I wanted right then was to run away, to find safe harbor, to go back home to Israel. The protective wall I'd built in my heart for five decades had been sundered, collapsed and reality's cruelty was coming at me headlong: my parents were no more, nor would I see them ever again.

Rain fell and drops mingled with my tears. Such intense longing for my parents, for my family: years had passed since I'd been in the yard, yet I could suddenly smell that unique scent of moist earth. The yard's appearance pained me. It was nothing like the way it had been in my childhood. The large yard had been split into two. Where we'd grown strawberries, a house now stood. Without our knowledge, without our agreement, we had 'donated' half a block of land for some Ukrainian family to build their home.

A strange feeling swept through me. This house, once bubbling with life, was empty of vitality now. Once a large family had lived here, celebrating Jewish festivals, sharing Shabbat every week, inviting countless people. A white tablecloth. Tall candlesticks with lit candles. Two freshly baked challah breads, beautifully braided and covered with a special white cloth.

I remembered the hustle and bustle which preceded Pessach as we took the special Pessach dishes down from the attic. How we cleaned every nook and cranny thoroughly, how we purchased the flat round matzah with a sense of awe and brought it home. Baked in small home bakeries, they remained untouched until the night that the festival began. How we, the children, would wait expectantly for the moment we could bite into them!

We children were outfitted head to toe in new clothes and would accompany Tateh to synagogue. By the time we were back, the table had been set, the aroma of traditional foods spreading through our home.

And I remembered how laundry had been hung in the yard. In winter's frost and snow, the sheets, pillowcases and sleeves of our dresses stiffened, sticking out, waving about in the breeze like ghosts in the day, scarecrows at night.

Going inside, my eyes scanned the interior for familiar objects that might remind me of the past. But there was nothing: only the walls were familiar. Closing my eyes, I imagined my parents and family; I could hear them talking. My heart skipped a beat. I was shaking.

Deep sorrow filled me; I did my best to hide my feelings. No one was aware of the emotions swirling inside. I went back to the yard. Vines still grew along the fence, clusters of unripe grapes hanging on stems. Sevluš was renowned for its wonderful quality grapes. As I walked about the house and the yard, my children filmed constantly: the facade, the pulley wheel, the yard, the garden, committing these slivers of my past to permanent memory.

I'd brought the family here: my two sons Tzvi and Gadi, my daughter Nurit, and Gadi's wife Valerie. Ilana, Tzvi's wife, had stayed home to care for their three boys: Boaz, aged nine; Yoav, seven; and Evyatar, just three months old. How I'd wanted my children to meet my parents and my parents to meet their grandchildren, but fate decided otherwise and it wasn't to be. How unfortunate that my dear husband Moshe hadn't lived long enough to join us.

Despite the situation's awkwardness, I felt closer to my parents here than anywhere else. I imagined us meeting in this house, even if just to bid our farewells, this time in a more pleasant manner because the way I'd been forced to leave them in Auschwitz always haunted me. I screamed in sorrow and pain, but no sound came out. I stood in the garden, my heart pounding as if it was booming out of my chest, but one could hear only birds chirping. My girlhood eyes gazed at the garden and suddenly the dam broke and a flood of memories washed ashore.

I remembered how we'd grown poppies among the cucumbers, potatoes, yellow beans. I remembered the cerise flower and how, when it ripened, we'd collect the poppy stems and leave them to dry in the sun. Then we snipped the hard crown off, emptied the contents into bowls, and sun-dried that again. The scent of Mameh's poppy seed cake in the oven, which stood outside in the yard, tickles my nose to this day.

As memories surfaced one after another, I felt an overwhelming urge to see the basement, where enamel vats of goose fat were stored in winter, where potatoes and carrots had been stored covered in earth to ensure their freshness. There was always a large barrel of cabbage fermenting into sauerkraut, as well as holding countless jars of fruit preserves and confitures lined up on the shelves. Backed against the wall was the storage cupboard.

The current owner invited us to sit in the garden, picking pears and apricots for us. Needing to reexperience the act of fruit picking, I walked up to the plum tree and plucked a couple off, crying, remembering better days that had disappeared forever.

Gadi quietly asked me where the box of money and jewelry had been buried in the garden before we were expelled. "On the other side of the fence, under the Ukrainian neighbor's house," I answered, making sure not to point but merely nod in that direction. Could they be there to this day, buried deep in the ground?

We spent about an hour at the house, following which I thanked the woman who was kind enough to let us in, walk around, film, and taste the fruit. We said goodbye and went back into the street.

In no time rumors of our visit had spread to neighbors. Across the road, people looking to be in their late sixties and early seventies had gathered. They'd known my parents and other Jews in the street. I was continuing to point out details to my children: the home of the Berger family, whose son Hananya now lived in Ashkelon and, next to it, the Liberman family. Not far away was the grocery belonging to a Jewish family: their daughter Leah had been my good friend. In the parallel street, I explained, the Junger family had lived: their daughters were now in Israel. Opposite them, the Stern family. The elderly neighbors confirmed everything I was saying.

As I was still fluent in Hungarian, I could easily converse with my home's new owner and the neighbors, and was happy that the conversation went smoothly. I translated the neighbors' comments from Hungarian to Hebrew, and my children's questions from Hebrew to Hungarian. One neighbor, who only spoke Russian, wanted to join, so I switched between three languages until I found myself talking to our Hungarian driver in Hebrew and my Hebrew-speaking children in Russian. We laughed about this together, which broke some of the tension.

I showed my children where the Junger family's home had stood. Their daughter, Rivka, had gone through Auschwitz with me. When Dr. Mengele separated Sheindy/Yaffa from me and I'd fainted out of sorrow and shock, Rivka, who'd arrived on the deportation ahead of me and worked in the kitchen, had brought me water to drink, some more to wash my face, and stood with me until I recovered. We photographed their home because I wanted to bring Rivka, who now lived in Bnei Brak, a souvenir picture.

Most of my parents' neighbors and friends had long since passed away, and I had no contact with the current neighbors. They were complete strangers to me. I sought friends, acquaintances, looking for people who'd known my parents because I was driven to share memories with someone right here in my city of birth. But I was surrounded by strangers, and felt like a stranger in my city.

From there we drove to Czech Street which, in my childhood, had been lined on both sides by massive, beautiful cherry trees. When their red and yellow fruit ripened, the flavor was amazing. But the trees had disappeared and the street had a sad, glum appearance.

Next, we headed to The Great Synagogue. Once again I was flooded by childhood memories. Tateh had worshipped here. I approached with mixed feelings. Today this beautiful synagogue is a sports hall, no external markings on the building to signify its original purpose, or that it was our city's pride and joy.

The building was neglected, time having peeled away layers of paint. Nurit, having already peeked inside, suggested I look in through the door but forewarned me: the space was a mess of broken benches and junk. I didn't look inside, lacking the emotional strength to view the destruction and abandonment.

Rubi Farkas told us that the community had decided to collect the names of all Jews still living in Sevluš, hoping that the total would justify a request that the authorities allow the reopening of the synagogue.

Across the road from the synagogue, the Sevluš Ghetto had been delineated. In it the suffering, torment, hunger and humiliation began. Here we Jews were isolated from other residents, locked up like caged animals, the non-Jews glaring at us over fences. Post-war, most of the older homes in the ghetto facing the road had been destroyed, replaced by apartment blocks looking like long train carriages, as well as a few separate, free-standing homes. No trace of the ghetto remained, no names or signs. But on the pharmacy wall at the street's furthest end we discovered a plaque in Russian, Hebrew and Hungarian:

A ghetto had existed in this quarter
From here our Jewish citizens were led
To the extermination camps in Spring 5704

The Jewish year 5704 corresponded to the Gregorian year 1944. The authorities had affixed this plaque in memory of the countless Jews deported and murdered in Auschwitz.

Next we went to the walled Sevluš Jewish cemetery. Entering through the gate, held closed with a scrap of barbed wire, we saw broken gravestones, others about to topple, and pieces of headstones scattered on the ground. Wildflowers and shrubs grew unimpeded among the graves but the names of the deceased were still visible. Cloudy skies grew darker, rain began falling in fine sheets. Walking among the gravestones, my heart cried: where was the gravestone indicating that my parents had ever lived? It was hard to accept.

Wanting to show my children where the torment began, we went to the train station where we'd been loaded on carriages: elderly and infants, men and women, pregnant women and the sick, along with whatever possessions we could carry on our backs, gendarmes with feathers in their caps hurrying us on, the long, seemingly endless line of people. Cries and screams had filled the air. We were going, but no one could say where.

I asked to drive slowly down the street leading to the station, searching for number 10, the Gross family's home, whose sons now lived in Netanya and who asked for a souvenir photograph. On the other side of the road there'd once been a flour mill. Now a large supermarket stood there: its shelves were empty. Waiting for abundance that would one day arrive?

No matter who I asked about buying a souvenir of Sevluš, my home town, the same answer came: "There's nothing to buy here." A postcard of the city? I asked. No, not even that. Such disappointment.

My skin goose bumped as we approached the train station. It was the last stop we shared in Sevluš with our parents. From here Sevluš Jews were sent to Auschwitz, to death by murder. As we stood there, a passenger train pulled in, as though adding weight to the truth of the past.

Gadi filmed the train pulling in. My children asked one question after another. They wanted to know the details. I showed them where the waiting room was; Nurit wanted to look inside but the door was locked. Through the window we saw a pile of junk inside. That's where we'd sat on the floor crowded on top of each other.

I remembered Mameh's words: "We won't be going home. We don't have a home anymore." I can still see the tears streaming down her face. I see Tateh trying to reassure her but he, too, is choked with tears. Their hands touched, their fingers interlocked. My sister and I huddled in the corner next to them, afraid to move, afraid to say a word.

Throughout, SS guards moved among us with sheets of paper containing 'lists of deportees,' but all they wanted to know was how many people could be shoved into a carriage. I remember them standing among us, talking, joking, laughing while we huddled on the floor, surrendered, defeated. They seemed so tall to me in their crisply starched uniforms and mirror-shined boots.

Splitting the air: the train's whistle as the train chugs slowly in. The waiting room doors open. "Everyone up!" the SS and guards shout at us. They hurry us because we aren't moving fast enough for their liking, it seems. "Schnell! Schnell! Raus!" comes the order. Faster. Out. Elderly people and children, frightened, are pushed towards the door. The guards help get us through the doors and onto the carriages by wielding their rifle butts.

Cattle car doors open. The entrance is very high up and difficult to board. Children are lifted in, elderly are tossed up and in like sacks of flour, losing their packages as they land with a thud. "Schnell! Schnell!!" There's no time. We need to hurry. An SS officer stands next to the carriage entrance counting. "Enough!" he shouts. "Close the doors! The carriage is full!"

A massive padlock which had hung on a hook on the door is used to lock us in. White chalk shows the number 85. That's the number of people in the carriage.

"Next carriage!" the SS officer orders. We're confused, panicked, barely make it up, then cower in a corner, shaking in fear in this midsummer as though it's midwinter. The metal doors slide shut. The padlock is set in place. Utter darkness fills the carriage. We are disconnected from the world.

Our tour of Sevluš has come to an end. We say goodbye to Rubi and thank him for accompanying us to the city's exit.

Turning back, I take a look at Sevluš, the dream I'd held for fifty years, now packed into three short hours. A last look at the city closes the circle for me. I am so grateful to my children for going on this journey with me, hand in hand, looking after me throughout this tough morning. Without them, I wouldn't have withstood it. I was also pleased that, at the very least, a decent, smiling woman lived in my family's home and received us graciously, letting us in the home, yard and garden.

Now I wanted to leave Ukraine as quickly as possible. My Sevluš, the one I'd known in childhood, was no more.

We drove back to Chap, stopping at a lone restaurant on the highway for coffee. The sign above the place advertised 'Espresso' but the liquid offered was black and bitter, made most likely from chicory. Sugar and milk or cream? Nowhere to be found.

We asked how much it was. "If you don't have coupons, I don't know how much to request," the owner said. Gadi gave the fellow a few dollars. Effusive thanks were forthcoming. The young fellow hugged Gadi and blessed him. We thought he'd start dancing any second, he was so overjoyed. Another three hours: that's how long it took to get through border control and back into Hungary.

Now there was only one circle left to close: a visit to Ohe, Germany.

For years I'd toyed with the idea of going back to visit the Lochte family. Twenty-four years after leaving the village I wrote to both the Lochte and Laupper families. Having no idea whether their children had remained in the village, I wrote to the village priest, asking him to forward the letter. How surprised I was when one day a response came from Mrs. Laupper, my sister's 'family.'

The letter was warm and friendly, asking how we were and whether we'd found our parents and siblings. She added that my adoptive mother had passed away some years ago and that Valter now ran his own farm. Right away I responded, adding a letter addressed to Valter and asking her to forward it to him. The letter said I'd be happy to correspond with him. No answer came back. For years, no mail was exchanged. Now, with a trip in the offing, the time had come to renew contact.

The international telephone exchange in Israel found Valter's phone number. It took two days for the exchange to locate the village of Ohe, and longer to find his number. I called. He answered. I explained who I was. It took a few moments for him to remember. Then he apologized.

"I was only eleven at the time."

"Yes, and I was barely sixteen. But we were very good friends."

"True, true. I remember you well."

I explained that I was planning to visit Germany with my family for three days in August and would love to come to Ohe and visit him.

"Where are you calling from?" he asked.

I answered. There was another silence. Then a question.

"Are you coming from Israel especially to visit me?"

"Yes," I said.

He would be very pleased to meet me, he said, and was looking forward to our arrival. Based on his response, I planned the Ohe part of our trip, having no idea what to expect and how he would receive me after so many years. Did he really remember me? I also had no idea how the family reacted among themselves or the hurt I'd cause them once I'd revealed my truth, my crime: I was Jewish.

We flew to Frankfurt on August 11, 1993, and from there to Hannover, picked up the prebooked rental car at the airport, then drove to Celle. There was plenty of time, so we decided to walk around the city, which I'd once known fairly well. Strolling up and down the main streets, I looked for the city hall which, at the time, is where we'd received certification that we were German refugees, along with identity cards, food cards, clothes and shoes. We did find the large, old, beautifully designed building that matched my description, but it now served as a museum. Valerie asked one of the employees if, fifty years earlier, it had been the town hall. "Yes!" came the answer.

I showed my children how we fled from there, gripping our certificates because one of the female clerks suspected us, noticing us speaking oddly accented German. From there I took my children to the old hospital, next to which a new modern hospital now stands, and explained that our cousin, who left the village, found work here. I showed my children where we fled when the head nurse said Mali was Polish and we couldn't possibly have been her sisters, as we'd claimed to be.

We decided on a snack and went into a café. Nurit went to the counter to order cakes. Among them she suddenly noticed a rhubarb pie and remembered my story of Mrs. Lochte sending me down to the basement to bring apples and rhubarb, and how I'd managed to get Valter to help me without him realizing it. To mark that memory, Nurit bought us rhubarb pie.

Germany was well-groomed, geraniums of many colors flowering in window pots and on bridge railings. The streets and pavements were clean, without even a single cigarette butt. It was all so sterile that it seemed people floated wherever they went and never touched the ground.

We decided to look for a Bed & Breakfast near Ohe. As we approached the village, we noticed a road sign: Garssen. Five hundred meters into the village we reached a junction. Stepping out of the car, I closed my eyes, running through how we walked through the village streets the night we arrived, having no idea which way to turn.

Windows of homes had been shut. Long icicles hung from rooftops. Trees, homes and streets were covered in snow so white that it blinded us. Smoke rose from house chimneys. No doubt the residents were sitting around tables for dinner. We were so tired that night, which occasionally forced us to stop.

Hunger gnawed at us. How we longed to hibernate through the winter and wake to a post-war spring! Sheindy, eyes brimming with despair, had asked: where to now? My answer? To the right, and maybe we'll get lucky and find something hot to drink tonight. Now here we were, right at that point, fifty years later.

Telling my children that we need to enter the street from the right, we'd barely walked a few steps and there was the village mayor's house, window boxes flowering abundantly, the yard full of flowers and shrubs. When we had visited this house countless times, the mayor always receiving us warmly, pleasantly, ready to help.

I remembered the first time we arrived in the village, standing at the door, frozen, shaking, only our eyes begging for help. The mayor's wife had invited us in. It had been so warm inside that the ice frozen in our clothes had begun to melt. Indeed she poured us hot drinks. We hadn't drunk or eaten anything warm for days.

From there I went in search of the refugees' house known by all at the time as the 'Judenheim,' the Jews' House. To this day I have no idea why it was so called. Its roof was high and strongly angled. Suddenly Gadi spoke.

"Imma, over there is the house you're looking for." He was some two hundred meters further down the street from the village mayor's home, but tall trees had hidden the building from view. Coming closer as my children filmed, Tzvi asked if I was sure this was the refugees' home.

A man in uniform, ranks on his epaulettes, stepped out. Noticing people gathering in front of his home, he asked how he might help us. I explained that I'd been a refugee here fifty years earlier, though I didn't add that I was Jewish, and told him that the building had housed refugees fleeing in fear of the conquerors.

In his forties, the man of course couldn't remember such events, but he was very courteous and called his wife. She hadn't lived in Garssen for many years but, as we chatted, she remembered that the building indeed had housed refugees during WWII. "My mother for sure could have helped you," she said, "but she passed away not long ago."

The man in uniform asked where we were from. Hearing me answer, "Israel," he raised an eyebrow, smiled, but said nothing. Then he opened the gate and invited us inside.

As we walked into the yard, I instantly recognized the well where we drew water, which meanwhile had been acknowledged as a historic relic. The large yard was filled with flowers, a lawn and tall trees, and was generally well-tended. Although it looked very different from back then, there was no doubt in my mind that this was the right place. Affixed to the building, a plaque noted that the building had been constructed in 1747 as 'a target practice club.'

I told the woman that I'd known the village mayor of back then well, but had forgotten his name. "Gustav Sohnemann," she said. I recalled that he lived on the other side of the road; she confirmed that. I also learned that he'd passed away at the good old age of 94 a mere two years earlier, and that his son now lived in the house.

The woman invited us in. She wanted to show me a booklet in which the mayor's photograph appeared during one of the target practice competitions. I said I'd like to copy his name correctly from the booklet. Instead, she gifted it to me. Although she invited us to coffee, we politely refused, explaining that we still needed to reach Celle and it was getting late. We wished the couple well and left.

Some two kilometers from Celle we found a hotel. From there I called Valter. He was quite surprised to learn we were so close to his village. We arranged to meet at 4 p.m. the next day. Wanting to take maximum advantage of the time we had available, we drove to Celle again, where I returned to the spot where I'd jumped from the train.

How drastically it had changed since then. Houses and shops had been built in the area, and it was hard to recognize key points. I went to the spot where I estimated the train had stopped, a little beyond the station, recalling our fatal decision to jump, how we'd begun running nowhere and anywhere, how Sheindy/Yaffa, her foot injured, ran in those wooden clogs without complaining once, snow clinging to the soles, causing us to stop every so often and with frozen fingertips, pry it off so that we could continue distancing as fast and far as possible.

On the way to Ohe we stopped near the forest where we escapees had rested. How exhausted we'd been, how wet and hungry, wanting to recover a little before moving on. I looked for, but couldn't find, the tree trunk we'd sat on back then. Moving among these very tall trees, I remembered how they'd sheltered us for several hours.

At the appointed time we drove into Ohe. Both sides of the road were still lined with tall trees, as it had been then. It was quiet, peaceful: people must have been taking their siesta nap, the famous German *Schlafstunde*. My heart began racing. I was getting overexcited. Looking around, the place had hardly changed since I'd left! Perhaps there were a few more houses. Nothing more.

A young man drove a tractor in our direction. We signaled, stopping him to ask where we'd find Valter's house. Not far off, it turned out. Going into the farm's yard, I noticed how clean and tidy it all was, although I also noticed an absence of animals: no cows, chicken, not even a dog. In my time, every farm had several laborers working for them, which included helping with the farm animals.

Going up to the front door, my eye caught Valter's name on a small board hung on the lintel. I became anxious: how would he receive me after so long? Would he remember me? Would he be pleasant or would this meeting be awkward? I rang the bell.

The door opened. There stood Valter, a huge smile on his

face. "Hilda!" he said, hugging and kissing me. Fifty years disappeared in the blink of an eye. There was an older Valter with the same grin of joy he'd always had when he saw me. Inviting us in, my children and I sat with him at the table. Conversation flowed easily and warmly.

"First things first," he said, opening a bottle of wine, "let's celebrate this occasion!" I apologized for my German being less fluent now, not having spoken it for five decades.

Valter immediately surprised me with a generous offer: to spend two months in the village polishing my German. We chatted, going back fifty years, comparing what we remembered of that time. I reminded him of his childhood. He was thrilled to talk about it.

That grin: suddenly he seemed like the mischievous young boy again. He remembered that my name had been listed as Herscowitz! Amazing! Imagine that detail staying in his mind all these years. A shiver of amazement and joy ran down my spine. My children were so surprised that they burst into laughter. Now we can call you Uncle Valter, they said.

Valter also remembered my long sleeves, which I'd never roll up. He remembered us going out riding, and being angry with me for not agreeing to go swimming with him in the stream: of course he never knew why I feared going swimming.

I reminded him of foods he loved and naughty things he did. During that period of the war, I said, kids weren't going to school and I was like an older sister, spending so much time with him. Mr. Lochte had been fifty when his son Valter was born, and there were almost no other children of that age with whom he could be friends and play.

He had a question for me, something he'd never understood: how did I get to the village of Ohe? I described our escape from the train that night with my sister and how we coincidentally ended up in Garssen, the Burgermeister taking care of us by giving us a place to stay that night and how, sometime later, he arranged for us to be placed in Ohe.

But Valter wanted to know more. "You said you're from Czechoslovakia, so how did you even get to Germany?" I couldn't believe my ears: he still hadn't connected me with the Holocaust!

So I explained that when the Germans invaded and conquered Europe, they deported all the Jews to Auschwitz, to the various concentration and death camps. My family was also deported, which is how I reached Auschwitz. I told him that my parents and the rest of my family were murdered and burned in the crematoria, and that my sister and I fled from the train intended to transport us from Guben to Bergen Belsen.

As soon as I said 'Auschwitz' he nodded. "Yes, now I understand," he said, then added, "but every place has its good people, and its evil ones." I chose not to react. He quickly moved onto a different topic.

Valter's parents had long since passed away and he was the only one left of his family. His wounded older brother Günter actually died in 1947. His other brother, Hans, whom I'd never met, had also passed away. His wife and children lived in the village of Schans, just across the border with The Netherlands. Valter's daughter had been killed in a car accident when she was twenty. He never spoke about his wife and I chose not to ask about what seemed like a sensitive issue. Living on his own in the village left him very lonely.

Valter invited us to a restaurant in the neighboring village. He was disappointed to hear that we'd only come for a short visit of several hours. Nonetheless, despite the pleasure and joy over our renewed contact, I could sense a touch of hesitation on his part, as though asking himself why I'd come, why I'd returned after so many years, what secret might I be harboring this time, or what surprises did I have lurking? Knowing that I was formally adopted by his parents, perhaps he wondered whether I'd returned to claim a share of the inheritance. It felt to me as though he was on the alert for the rabbit I might suddenly pull out of the hat and my true reasons for being in the village would be disclosed.

When I asked why there were no animals on the farm, he explained that it simply didn't pay to maintain the cowsheds and chicken coops. The young generation preferred other professions and abandoned agriculture. Some farmers still worked their land, others rented out holiday bungalows, or recast their homes as vacation and tourism options. Valter had turned to raising pure-bred horses, adding that he'd recently won prizes for his horses at a show in Belgium, selling three, a worthy achievement.

My children expressed their interest in visiting the stables. Valter gave us a guided tour, proudly presenting the beautiful creatures. He took an interest in Israel's political and economic climate, plying us with plenty of questions. We did our best to answer.

Then I asked if it was possible to visit the Lochte home. He walked over there with us. We didn't go inside, just stood in the yard. I pointed out my room's window to my children. Memories bubbled up: the stables, the shed filled with dairy cows, the cackling of chickens, and the milk wagon harnessed to horses and bringing laborers at dawn into the fields for a day's work.

Now there was a blanket silence broken only by a lone tractor's engine chugging along, disrupting the *Schlafstunde*. I wanted to see the Laupper home where my sister had been hosted. Mr. Laupper was still alive, explained Valter, but he'd sold his farm and now lived in a different city. We could do no more than take photos of the house as keepsakes.

I invited Valter to visit Israel and be a guest in my home. Usually, he explained, he didn't travel much, having no one he could really rely on to take care of the horses, but he thanked me graciously. It may take some time, he added, but who knows? Maybe he'd surprise me one day!

It was time to say goodbye. Valter stood in the yard waving until our car disappeared down the village road.

And so another part of my life came to a close: I'd seen Ohe once more, fifty years later.

52 YEARS LATER

In Spring of 1996, my son Tzvi and I took the journey to Auschwitz-Birkenau. I decided to go back there and light a memorial candle for my parents and family members who perished in the death camps. I felt a deep need to recite 'Kaddish,' the Mourner's Prayer, for their souls, the least I could do for them.

It was cold and gloomy the day we arrived. The same gate stood at the entrance: Arbeit Mach Frei. The same tall chimney stood there, but no longer belching tongues of fire and pillars of thick black smoke as the bodies of Nazi victims burned. The same threatening watch towers were still in place. The same barbed wire fence, with signs: 'Beware. High Voltage.' And the same railroad tracks on which trainloads of Jewish families were brought to the slaughter.

Memories I'd repressed for decades rushed to the fore. Closing my eyes, I once again became that teenager in the gray dress, my head shaven, alone in a death camp. Abandoned. I shook and trembled. And suddenly realized I was no longer alone. Thousands of Jewish youth from Israel and the Diaspora were standing there with me. In our blue wind jackets emblazoned with a Star of David, we were part of the 'March of the Living' program memorializing victims of the Shoah, the Holocaust. Blasts on the shofar were sounded. I joined young Israelis walking in the footsteps of the past.

During the ceremony at Birkenau, a feeling of unity swept

through us. We were part of one family, standing quietly, only the cantor's voice praying the 'El Maleh Rahamim' prayer cutting through the absolute silence. Tears fell from my eyes: if anywhere, this was the place to cry. And to shout: Never Again! In my mind I see my parents standing at the gate, frightened, dogs barking wildly. They are confused by the SS officers' shouts. Is this a dream or reality, I wonder? But here in this miserable place I discover hope. Yes, I was expelled from my home, from my city, my family was murdered but, like the proverbial phoenix, I raised my head high and, with the help of my wonderful husband, Moshe Kan-Tor (formerly Kantrezi), born to a Hadera founding family and the support of my dear children, I learned to love again and be joyful.

From the moment I agreed to go on the trip to Auschwitz, nightmares once again began to overwhelm me, and I was forced to draw on all my strength to restrain myself from changing the plans. Thousands visit Auschwitz every year, survivors with their children, with their grandchildren, to find some closure. Visiting the museum left its mark on us, dampening and sorrowing our mood. Seeing the piles of shoes left us breathless and speechless: thousands of pairs: for children aged three, four or five; for infants and toddlers who trusted the adults around them; for children still unable resist or even formulate questions, who were extinguished in an instant, the wicks of their lives snuffed out.

Hair. Tons of it. Held in massive net holders. Curly, blond, long, and dark, and white elderly hair, braids, some tied together with ribbons. Whose were they? Little girls? Teens? I can see them weeping as their hair is first cut, and then their heads shaved. I can't shake the image loose: what happened to my own hair? What did the Germans do with it? Perhaps mine is in this enormous pile, looking at me right now? Asking: "Hey you, weren't we yours once upon a time? Why were we separated from you?" My tears surged when I thought of these things. But

I make a conscious decision: you belong to the past, whereas I belong to the future.

These are more of these museum exhibits: reconstructed crematoria ovens which make my skin crawl; and hundreds of memorial candles, burning next to the wall of death. How many Jewish prisoners were exterminated at this accursed wall?

Organizers of the 'March of the Living' handed out small wooden strips on which we wrote the names of our loved ones. These were then pushed into the ground, in their memory. Brilliant, white snow covered the ground. Bending down, with quivering hands, I raised a clump of snow, bringing it to my mouth as I'd done in those days when I was forced to take part in the procession, the 'March of Death.'

Delegations were readying to leave Birkenau. Dozens of large Israeli flags were raised high and fluttered. Every participant held a small Israeli flag. What a stunning, heartwarming sight. I wanted everyone to see how we'd raised our heads and, despite their attempts to kill us, we survived and remained alive.

We stood before a monument commemorating the victims. I glanced at the buildings, the barracks, the crematorium, the showers, the mounds of shoes, hair, glasses, suitcases and the rest of it, evidence of this German genocide for thousands to witness.

Thinking about my escape from the death camps, I wondered: was it destiny, or luck? Had I been entrusted with carrying on my family's bloodline? My parents surfaced again in my mind: I imagined that terrible moment when they were herded into the shower block, unable to breathe yet not comprehending why, not expecting the cruelty of dying by being gassed, falling dead on each other in piles of naked, lifeless corpses. The image froze the blood in my veins.

Leaving via Birkenau's gateway, an intense feeling of isolation and orphanhood filled me. Fifty-two years had passed. I'd buckled down and gotten on with life, coping with life's ebb and flow, but now I needed to close that circle. I felt an obligation towards my parents, for whom I never sat 'Shivah,' the week-long mourning period according to Jewish custom. On returning to Israel I would fulfill that commandment, I decided. I was uncertain how to do it, or when, or whether I should do it so many years later.

Dusk began to color the sky. Before leaving this horrific place, I muttered a few words of farewell. "Rest in peace, my dearest parents; rest in peace, my brother and sisters; rest in peace, my little niece. May all my family rest peacefully. My dear parents, I returned to Auschwitz to redeem your memories. May you find tranquility beneath the wings of Shechinah, God's Divine Presence, Amen."

From Auschwitz we traveled to Kraków-Płaszów where I stood, once again, in the concentration camp built on a Jewish cemetery. A sudden alertness came about, together with a deep sense of inner emptiness. My mind was whirring: what were these sensations telling me? Suddenly I realized: the Poles had plowed the earth, erasing all traces of the crime! They demolished the existence of thousands of prisoners who suffered horribly in this camp. Only the broad steps leading to the living quarters remained. Of the entire camp, no more than two headstones were left, some a distance away, attesting silently to the past's violent atrocities.

For years I'd wondered how far we had actually walked on the Death March. Now, as part of the March of the Living, I decided to check. Tzvi, studying the map of Poland, calculated that the distance between Greenberg, its post-war name Zielona Góra, to Guben totaled 120 kilometers. We marched that distance fifty-two years earlier, in the dead of winter, through thick snow, in icy cold temperatures, flimsy clothing, hungry, thirsty, weary and lost. We marched through forests and fields and along winding paths. For eight or nine days we marched until, exhausted physically and mentally, we reached the concentration camp in the city of Guben. I thought of the many, many women who didn't last this inhumane cavalcade, falling victim to Nazi cruelty.

Again the memories arise and I have to fight not to break down. Twice I'd been in Auschwitz, and twice I'd come out of the place on my own two legs. Not many were privileged with the same fate. Most who left Auschwitz went to forced labor camps, where they died from starvation, disease and being overworked, or were sent straight to the crematorium.

They say that time heals all wounds, but this wound is too deep and painful to ever heal. These scars can never be erased and, nevertheless, I learned to live for the present and the future.

And this is how: I have six grandchildren. My son Tzvi and his wife Ilana have three boys, Boaz, Yoav and Evyatar. My daughter Nurit has a son, Nadav. My son Gadi and his wife Valerie brought twin daughters, Sarah and Ayala, into the world just two weeks before our trip to Auschwitz. Together, they are like a battalion of witnesses proudly declaring that, despite it all, the chain of life continues, and the people of Israel lives. Am Yisrael Chai!

And here my story both ends yet continues into the future.

A RECKONING

My parents were taken from Sevluš in 1944 and sent straight to the crematoria.

My older sister, Rozie, was taken from Bratislava to Auschwitz in 1941 because she wouldn't separate from her only son, Moshe, nicknamed Miki, aged 8. Both were sent directly to the crematoria.

Rozie's husband, my brother-in-law, Zoli Adler, returned from Auschwitz to Bratislava and, in 1950, emigrated to Israel. He later remarried and had a son named Moshe (Miki), may he enjoy long life. In 1952 he was a guest at my wedding, which brought us all great joy.

My brother, Zeril-Hersh, was taken from Bratislava to Auschwitz in 1941 and murdered there.

My sister, Feigie, was taken from Bratislava to Auschwitz in 1941 and, from what I had heard, died there of typhus.

My two sisters, Zahava (Goldie) and Hannah, were in Budapest during the war. They worked in the Jewish hospital as nursing assistants, which enabled them to survive. When the war ended, they joined the Hashomer Hatzair Jewish youth movement, joining the kibbutz that consolidated in Bucharest.

Zahava emigrated to Israel on January 2, 1946, on the 'Enzo Sereni' refugee ship. In Israel she married and raised a family.

Hannah emigrated to Israel in 1947 on the 'Knesset Yisrael' refugee ship with her Hashomer Hatzair friends who formed the 'First of May' kibbutz. It later changed its name to Ga'aton. Hannah married and raised a family.

My younger sister, Sheindy/Yaffa joined the Aliyat HaNo'ar (Youth Emigration) group in Budapest, and emigrated to Israel in 1948 on the famed 'Exodus' refugee ship, representing the exodus from Europe. She, too, married and raised a family.

After the war I joined the Hashomer Hatzair movement's 'First of May' kibbutz consolidating in Budapest. The kibbutz group set sail on the 'Bracha Fuld' refugee ship in 1947. Upon it eventually reaching Israel, the kibbutz changed its name to Kibbutz Yas'ur.

Members of the First of May kibbutz also established Kibbutz Yehiam.

In Israel I met a born and bred Israeli, a young man named Moshe Kan-Tor. He was the son of one of the founders of the city of Hadera, the large Kantrezi family which, at the time, had settled into three small rooms in Hadera's famous inn. We married in 1952 and raised our family.

My cousin Mali, who left Germany right after its liberation in 1944, returned to her family in the USA.

Concerning Mali's friend, Marika, we heard nothing further after our ways parted in the German village of Garssen.

THE SECOND GENERATION SPEAKS

For us, this is an intensely personal story. It details our otherwise very private mother's history of survival and resourcefulness. It has only now become known to us, leaving us amazed at how she kept it hidden for fifty years. We read it, and wondered how it played out. On one hand, we know that every word written here is truth. On the other, it is almost incomprehensible, skating closer to fiction than factual. But as happens so frequently, fact surpasses the imagination.

I accompanied my mother to all the locations which the book described: from the home where she was born, to the Auschwitz-Birkenau and Kraków-Płaszów extermination camps, and to the village of Ohe and city of Celle in Germany. In Ohe we met our 'adopted uncle,' Valter Lochte.

We saw these places with our own eyes yet, at each moment we found the experiences and events that made up our mother's adolescence hard to believe. This is why we can well imagine the astonishment that a reader, not having been there, might feel.

Until she began writing, our mother rarely mentioned her story of survival. Only once she began writing down the chain of events did we discover, for the first time, how they shed new light on aspects of her personality, allowing us to better understand the source of these traits that had always characterized her: determination, ingenuity, and self-discipline.

Although on a personal and family level the Shoah (Holocaust) was not a constantly referenced part of our upbringing, something of its influence did seep into our lives. I remember that during my week-long combat training bootcamp, which required me to sign on for an extra two years of military service, I was asked in the interview if there was a chance that I'd choose a military career.

When I answered in the negative, the interview asked: "If that's the case, why are you willing to sign on for the extra two years? Isn't that a waste of your time?" My gut-instinct response surprised even me: "My mother was a survivor of Auschwitz. It's my duty to do my part in ensuring that those events never reoccur."

As my mother reached the book's end, I joined her on the trip to Poland as part of the important venture known as 'March of the Living.' We spent a week visiting the locations mentioned in this book and, together with her, I experienced the sorrow and the angst, as well as the emotional highs and lows. Our mother was able to talk openly, to describe what we were seeing and the events that shaped her life, and I could see her weeping yet gazing lovingly at the long line of Jewish youth carrying the Israeli flag. I thought it imperative to tell them that every survivor has his or her unique personal story, and to emphasize that that, in most of these cases, the truth of how they survived seems more unbelievable than anyone's wildest imagination.

We, the survivors' children, absorbed the essence and spirit of what our parents had underwent and heard the stories firsthand. This book is being published so that people who have never had direct contact with those who experienced the Holocaust can also "Remember, and Never Forget."

THE THIRD GENERATION SPEAKS

Our **grandmother was** a European lady. For example, she had business cards – her name, address and phone number – which she would hand to the neighborhood grocer, the butcher, or to the dry cleaner. She spoke Hungarian, and everything with her was meticulous. The dining table was made of solid wood, the wine glasses were made of crystal, the hair was dyed and the haircut was elegant, always with earrings and rings and bracelets, smiling generously with red lipstick. She lived in a spacious house, a hedge raised up in the front and back yards. Buried underground was a cellar with stocks of food, sugar and salt and tins of cans. I would hide there as a child.

When a war broke out in Israel, missiles were launched into the city where Grandma lived. Our parents were abroad and therefore my eldest brother, who was already a discharged soldier, was sent to bring her to us. "No way," she replied firmly, "I ran away from home once, I won't run away again." He told her that our younger brother was afraid: "Come for his sake." Grandma came to her senses, disappeared into her room and returned with a small suitcase. Her things and clothes were already packed in the suitcase, she was ready.

Eighty-plus years old, still driving her Suzuki, a thin Montana cigarette dangling from the corner of her mouth. Once, on her way to tell high school students her life story, she was involved in a car accident. Frightened, I rushed to the hospital and found her there, with the same red lipstick and pearl necklace, playing cards with the medical staff. She proudly told her new fans that her grandson is a computer student at the Hebrew University, and she asked me with the same generous smile: "What are you doing here, Yoav? Don't you have another lady to visit tonight?"

I was a teenager when I read this book, when I read my grandmother's stories from the Holocaust. I was amazed because she was my age at the time, so determined and brave, a hero. Her history, consciously and subconsciously, seeped through the cracks of reality and shaped my life as well. As great as the tragedy that befell her, so was her devotion to life. I am writing these lines here because a sixteen-year-old girl held her little sister's hand and chose life. How strange and miraculous is this thought.

She passed away in her sleep. She spent her last day in a beauty salon, with manicure and pedicure treatments and a new haircut, as if she was dressing up for a trip to the next world. I miss her a lot. I imagine myself visiting her like I used to, the tea in the china cups and the roasted peanuts on the table, she lights a cigarette, and I remind her that it's not healthy, and she looks at me with a smile and blows a cloud of smoke from her mouth: "I won't be dying young anymore." I would tell her that in the high school where I taught, I told the students about her journey of survival, and that there was a new immigrant in the class who came from a town near Sevluš, her town. I would show her pictures of the granddaughter she didn't know, and the two great-grandchildren born to her in recent years, and how much they look like her. This time, I am the one who proudly presents her with my business card: "Doctor Kan-Tor," she surely would have asked with the same smile, "Don't you have another lady to visit tonight?"

ACKNOWLEDGMENTS

I wish to express my deepest thanks to all who offered their time and assistance, commented and invested effort, provided details, and supported me throughout the writing of this book.

To Haimeh Cohen, who never tired of listening to my deliberations, and guided me so well with his attention and understanding.

To *Klara Karni* for her dedication and insight.

To *Noa Paternak* and *Einat Leibowicz* who suffered through the many ups and downs.

To *Ruti ben-Shaul* for her professional assistance.

To my dear children, who encouraged me throughout with love.

And special thanks to my dear husband, the late *Moshe*, who did not see the book come to fruition but without whose encouragement and patience it would never have been documented.

Finally, to *Yoram Taharlev* for his professionalism and generosity.

Made in the USA
Monee, IL
15 April 2025

15848922R20132